Dear Reader,

Do *you* have a secret fantasy? Everybody does. Maybe it's to be rich and famous and beautiful. Or to start a no-strings affair with a sexy mysterious stranger. Or to have a sizzling second chance with a former sweetheart.... You'll find these dreams—and much more—in Temptation's exciting new yearlong promotion, Secret Fantasies!

Award-winning author Lisa Harris contributes this month's story, *The Tempting*. Heroine Carol Glendower wants her husband back...*alive*. Evan was handsome, sexy, perfect. But he's gone now. Carol must risk *everything* to fulfill her secret fantasy. Dare she?

In the coming months look for Secret Fantasies books by Regan Forest, Kate Hoffmann and Tiffany White. Please write and let us know how you enjoyed the "fantasy."

Happy Reading!

The Editors

c/o Harlequin Temptation
225 Duncan Mill Road
Don Mills, Ontario M3B 3K9
Canada

Dear Reader,

When the Harlequin editors approached me about writing a Secret Fantasies book, I was delighted, for I'd long had an unusual story in mind.

It all began with a vivid mental picture. A black cat walked soundlessly across the floor of a deserted, dusty room and disappeared beneath an antique bed.

A worn tapestry hung over the bed's edge, touching the floor. A young woman came after the cat, wanting to retrieve it from beneath the bed. But when she lifted the tapestry throw, she saw something both unexpected and unearthly...and she knew (and I knew) that her life was changed forever. This is her story.

I hope you enjoy reading *The Tempting* as much as I enjoyed writing it. And always remember, if you love enough, *anything* is possible in this world.

Sincerely,

Lisa Harris

"I worried about you the whole time you were away," Evan said.

"Something might have happened to you," he whispered against her hair. "I couldn't stand it."

Carol pressed her mouth to the hollow of his throat. His skin tasted clean and warm and slightly salty.

"What about you?" she murmured. "What if something happened to you?"

"Nothing's going to happen to me." Evan sealed the vow with a hungry kiss. "I love you too much. I'll always come back. No matter what."

She could feel the vital power in his shoulders. And his arms were strong around her....

Then she woke—it was only a dream. Evan *had* left her. And he wasn't coming back. *Couldn't* come back.

The question was: If he did, could she give up everything just to be with him?

Lisa Harris has loved the combination of fantasy and fear since being deliciously scared, at the age of four, by the witch in Walt Disney's *Snow White*. The first story she ever wrote—in grade one—was about a haunted castle. Interestingly, her husband was born on Halloween! She has published over thirty books, including romances, mysteries and humorous fiction, as well as nonfiction.

Books by Lisa Harris

HARLEQUIN TEMPTATION
485—UNDERCURRENT
495—TROUBLE IN PARADISE

HARLEQUIN ROMANCE
3304—I WILL FIND YOU!

Don't miss any of our special offers. Write to us at the following address for information on our newest releases.

Harlequin Reader Service
U.S.: 3010 Walden Ave., P.O. Box 1325, Buffalo, NY 14269
Canadian: P.O. Box 609, Fort Erie, Ont. L2A 5X3

THE TEMPTING
LISA HARRIS

Harlequin Books

TORONTO • NEW YORK • LONDON
AMSTERDAM • PARIS • SYDNEY • HAMBURG
STOCKHOLM • ATHENS • TOKYO • MILAN
MADRID • WARSAW • BUDAPEST • AUCKLAND

To Cheops the Great—
He finally got it in print

ISBN 0-373-25634-5

THE TEMPTING

1

THE BLACK CAT CAME into her life as quietly as a shadow, and that was why she named him Shadow. She opened her front door one morning, and there he stood, large and sleek and green eyed.

He walked into the house as casually and confidently as if it were his destiny to be there. He never meowed or purred or made a sound of any kind.

Carol tried to find his owner by advertising in the newspaper and sending notices to all the local veterinarians. No one responded, so she assumed the cat had simply been abandoned.

"I seem to have a cat," she told Charles when he took her to dinner Friday night. "He's adopted me."

Charles gave her a sympathetic look, an encouraging smile. He always treated her as though she were a convalescent, a woman so fragile she might break.

"That's good," he said with a nod. "That's probably good for you. Having a pet."

She felt the smile freeze on her face. Charles was always searching for signs of recovery in her. To him, the cat could not simply be a cat; it had to be an emblem, a symbol that she was getting "better."

Charles was a tall, rather soft-looking man, whose curly hair was thinning. His blue eyes were usually full of concern for her, and sometimes, like tonight, too much concern.

"He's not really a pet," she said, hating the edge in her voice. "He's not affectionate. It's as if he belongs to the house, not to me."

Charles's fleshy face took on an expression of even greater tenderness. He smiled. "I'm just glad you're taking an interest in something," he said.

Oh, God, what's wrong with me? she wanted to cry out. *Why does his kindness always offend me? Why do I resent him so much?*

But the answer to that was as simple as it was harsh. Charles, worshipful and boring, was alive. But Evan, who'd been laughing and irreverent and whom she had loved with all her soul, was dead.

Evan had been a microbiologist, as she was. They'd met when they were both working at the University of Nigeria. Both had been on leave from their own universities, he from California, she from Illinois.

She'd come back to the States first, wearing his wedding ring. She was to pick their house and have it ready when he rejoined her two months later.

It had been easy for him to find a university position in Chicago. He'd been so brilliant that almost any job he'd wanted was his for the asking.

She'd bought the house in the suburbs, an eccentric, rambling old thing that she'd known he would love. But he never joined her, never lived in it. Instead, he'd died of a new strain of virulent African fever.

He'd been among the university scientists trying to isolate the lethal virus that had suddenly arisen and begun to decimate the Niger Plateau. Three of the lab workers had died of it, and Evan was one.

They'd cremated him, as befitted a plague victim—on his wrist was the silver ID bracelet she'd given him as a wedding present. Because government red tape would not allow his remains to be shipped home, his ashes and a few charred drops of silver were scattered in the waters of the Slave Coast, west of the Niger Delta.

That was more than a year ago. She still lived in the strange, rambling old house. And here was Charles, waiting for her to stop mourning Evan and get on with life.

"Has anyone looked at the house this week?" Charles asked, refilling her wineglass. She knew he was eager for her to sell the place. He thought it kept her chained to the past.

"No," she said as levelly as she could. "It's just too weird, too eccentric."

In truth, she probably could have sold the place a dozen times over if only she lowered the asking price, but she kept it high because she really couldn't bear to part with the house. It was one of the few physical links she had with Evan.

"It can't be good for you," Charles said, "knocking around alone in that monstrosity. You could rent it out. Get a place closer to the university."

"I'm not alone," Carol said. "I've got the cat."

"O'Donnell wants out of the city and into the suburbs," Charles said. "He thinks it'd be better for his kids. He'd rent it from you in a minute."

O'Donnell was a new colleague of theirs in the biology department. He taught botany and had a large, unruly family of children, six of them. He hinted constantly that he and his wife needed a place exactly like hers.

Six children would fill the old place with life. The children would be raucous and vital and turn the house into a real home. Their clamoring voices would drive away its silence.

Yet she could not relinquish the place. She supposed it was selfish or perverse of her, but she could not. She had once expected her own children to fill it, hers and Evan's.

"No" was all she said.

Charles mercifully changed the subject, turned it to departmental gossip. She was relieved, because she could respond mechanically to small talk, almost without thinking. She could pretend to enjoy herself.

Later he drove her back to the university. He walked her to her car, put his hands on her shoulders and kissed her good-night.

His lips were soft, warm, moist and undemanding. Six months ago, he had asked permission for this intimacy. She had allowed him, but she took his kisses as if they were medicine.

How strange, she always thought, to have his lips and not Evan's upon her own. Evan's kisses had been like delicious, life-giving fire, but Charles's were lukewarm water that nourished nothing.

Yet she forced herself to go through the motions. She placed her hands lightly on Charles's upper arms. She kept her face tilted up to his.

"Good night, Carol." He whispered the words against her lips, and his breath smelled of wine and pumpkin pie. "Drive carefully."

She smiled. "Of course. You, too. Thanks for a lovely evening."

She disengaged herself from him, let him help her into her car. He stood watching protectively, until she started her car and safely exited the lot.

She made her way to the highway and switched on her cassette player. She always played the same tape—the one that had been Evan's favorite. It was full of songs about undying love, love that could not end.

DR. CAROL GLENDOWER was not quite twenty-nine years old, and people made a point of telling her she was too young to spend the rest of her life mourning.

Indeed, nature appeared to have designed her for high spirits, not for grieving. Her hair, a shining red gold, was her most distinctive feature, and she had a redhead's fair coloring, with freckles dancing across her nose and cheekbones.

Her eyes were large and dark gray, as beautiful as they were alert. Her auburn brows were wing shaped, and set at a mischievous tilt. Her mouth was full and seemed formed to smile.

Evan had told her he'd fallen in love with her the moment she'd walked into the microbiology lab at Ibadan. "It was like in the song," he said. "'You smiled, and my heart fell down at your feet. I was yours.'"

She'd heard about this American man sojourning at Ibadan, of course. Dr. Evan Glendower's special area of interest was human disease viruses, and he was in Nigeria primarily to study mutations in yellow fever.

As young as he was, only thirty-three, he was already known as one of the best and brightest in his field. She had come to Ibadan feeling more than a little intimidated by his reputation.

Of course she had expected he would be brilliant. She hadn't expected him to be tall and handsome and sexy, as well. He stood a little over six foot two. His shoulders were wide, his chest broad and his hips narrow.

He had wavy brown hair that tended to fall over his brow, and he always seemed to need a haircut, but that was all right—he looked good that way. His eyes were full of life and wit and were as blue as the hot Nigerian sky at noon.

He'd been standing with his back to her as she entered the lab. When he'd turned, and her eyes met the startling blue of his, it was as if something clicked into place in the universe, and suddenly she was raised, breathless, to a new level of being.

They simply stared at each other for a long moment. She *knew* immediately. So, he later said, did he. It was as though in those first wordless seconds, they held a silent conversation, filled with wonder.

It's you, she'd thought. *You exist. I've found you.*

And you, he'd seemed to say. *Yes. I've found you, too.*

Until that moment, she hadn't believed in romantic love, and certainly not in love at first sight. Such feelings were only imagined by songwriters and filmmakers, a pretty fiction that no sane adult could accept.

But there they were, the two of them, strangers who were not strangers in the least. She'd been waiting for him all her life, even if she hadn't known it. He smiled at her as if he'd just had the same realization about her.

He said the most extraordinary thing. He said, "Our kids will ask us about this again and again."

And smiling back helplessly, she'd nodded.

"We were engaged," he later said, laughing, "from the moment we met."

They married a week later. Their love affair was so intense, so all-consuming, that people said it couldn't last. But they both knew it was going to last forever.

She loved him so much that sometimes it scared her. Marrying him seemed almost a mere formality; she had felt wedded to him from the beginning of time.

His contract in Nigeria was slightly longer than hers, and she could hardly bear to leave him ten months later. The two-month wait for him to return to the States appeared an eternity, but she told herself that she was not really away from him, not in her heart. He was like a part of herself.

When he died, she felt as though most of her had died with him. She still wore his wedding ring. It was a two-carat green garnet he had bought for her in Tanzania, long after the wedding. They had been in too great a hurry to shop for rings when they wed.

Tanzania, she always thought with a pang when she looked at the green stone. They had camped at the top of an extinct volcano, now lush with grass. The next morning, they'd awakened in their sleeping bag to find themselves surrounded by clouds, as if they were in heaven.

In the distance, they heard elephants trumpeting, a primitive, magical sound. Evan unzipped the sleeping bag, and naked, they lay atop it, making sweet, mad love in the cool clouds.

She could still recall the texture and heat of his skin beneath her fingers, recall the feel of him so clearly that it made her ache. She imagined the weight of his body on hers, and how it had filled her with desire. She could remember how eager and ardent his mouth was on her face, her body.

While she was in the States and he was in Africa, they ran up terrible phone bills. They wrote each other wildly erotic letters full of pet names and private jokes. They planned their future.

She'd sent him at least a hundred pictures of their house and described it in lavish detail.

"You'll love it," she'd told him over the phone when she'd found it. "It's crazy. Like something the Addams family might live in. It's got six bedrooms. One is up in this octagonal tower thing. It's huge, and in the middle it's got a built-in bed on a sort of a platform."

He enumerated the things he intended to do to her in that bed, and she mentioned a few ideas of her own. They'd laughed together conspiratorially.

"It sounds great," he said. "Six bedrooms is perfect. Four for the kids, one for company, one for us. The tower with the built-in bed will be ours. I just hope it's built well, because it's going to see a lot of action!"

She'd laughed again.

She'd been moving her things into the house when he'd gotten sick. She had only a few pieces of furniture and was buying as little as possible before he returned. The rest they planned to purchase when they were together again.

He'd phoned on a Thursday evening, not sounding like himself. He said he had the very devil of a headache and was worn out.

She'd felt alarmed. He was never sick, never worn out. The Abuju fever virus was deadly, and she'd been worried when he'd first told her he'd be working with it. She was suddenly frightened again, deeply so.

But he'd joked that he was indestructible and made her believe it. He'd joked, too, about their tower room with its immense, immovable bed. "Oh, we'll move it, all right," he'd teased.

It was the last time she was to hear his voice.

She could not reach him by phone on Friday night, and she'd panicked, calling one of his fellow researchers, Dr. Akinyere Sales. Evan was in the hospital, Sales had told her, with a fever of 107.

Sales said he would call as soon as there was any change. For two days she'd stayed by her newly installed phone, afraid to call, full of superstitious dread. She couldn't sleep, couldn't eat.

On Sunday morning, there was a knock at her door. She opened it and found the gray-haired department chairman, Dr. Ethan Garrett, standing there. His lean face was grim.

And she knew what he had come to tell her. Evan was dead, and she felt as if her own life had ended.

When Sales finally phoned her, he was so shaken he could barely speak. He said Evan's last rational thoughts were about the silver ID bracelet, her gift to him.

"Don't let anybody take it from me," he'd made Sales promise. He died wearing it, Sales told her. It would be on his wrist when they cremated him.

On the day they burned his body, she walked up the stairs to the tower bedroom and locked the door. Then she put the key in her pocket and descended the stairs again.

She drove to Lake Michigan and took a long, lonely walk along its shore. When evening fell, she took the key from her pocket, looked at it for a long time, then threw it as far out into the water as she could. She stood staring at the darkening waves and listening to their cold hiss.

Only then did she cry.

IT WAS snowing outside. It seemed to have been snowing for weeks, months, aeons.

"You should give Charles a chance," said Carol's friend Veronica. They sat together in the student union, drinking coffee. "He's adored you for years."

"For years" meant since before Carol had gone to Nigeria. She and Charles had joined the faculty at the same time. He and she had both lost their mothers that year, and they had sympathized with each other. Although she hadn't meant for it to happen, he'd become smitten with her and had made no secret of it then or now.

"I am giving him a chance," Carol said. "He's taking me out again on Friday."

Veronica was a tall and beautiful black woman. She was an assistant dean, and unlike some campus administrators, she always said what she thought in no uncertain terms.

"He's always taking you out," Veronica said. "When are you going take him in?"

"What do you mean?" asked Carol, uneasy.

"I mean—take him into your life, your feelings, your bed?"

"My bed?" Carol repeated. The thought of making love to Charles seemed ludicrous and slightly obscene. *"Charles?"*

"Yes, Charles. What's wrong with him? He's bright, he's dependable, he's crazy about you."

Carol didn't meet Veronica's eyes. "He isn't very exciting," she hedged.

"Exciting?" Veronica said with a snort. "You can have exciting. My first husband was exciting. He was so exciting I used to have to call the police. Trust me, honey. Dependable is better."

Veronica's first husband had been a handsome firebrand who'd turned out to be both abusive and unfaithful. She was married now to an insurance executive who was short, round, bald, jolly and worshipped the ground she walked on.

"I just don't feel that way about Charles," Carol said.

"Well, you ought to let yourself feel 'that way' about somebody. You're going to wake up one of these days middle-aged with nobody to keep you company except yourself. One is a lonesome number. You're not meant to stay alone like this."

Carol managed a stiff little smile. "I'm not alone. I have my cat."

The cat, she thought, troubled. Shadow. It had been a month now since Shadow had appeared, green eyed and silent, on her doorstep.

"I thought the cat was lost."

"He turned up again," Carol said.

"Where was he?"

"I don't know."

She stared moodily into her untasted coffee. She needed to talk to someone about the cat, but the prospect frightened her a bit. She decided she would try.

"Twice he's disappeared like that," Carol said. "He was gone for two days the first time. A week the second."

"Hmm," Veronica said. "He must have somebody else who feeds him and treats him nice. Tomcats are like that. Human and feline."

Carol frowned slightly. "No. He wasn't out. He was in."

"What?" said Veronica. "How could he be lost while he's inside?"

Carol felt a bit light-headed, almost giddy. Slowly she lifted her gaze and stared into Veronica's dark eyes.

"It sounds strange. But he hasn't gone outside since snow's been on the ground. He doesn't like to touch it. He stays in. All the time."

Veronica's expression grew guarded, thoughtful. "So you're saying he got lost inside your house?"

Carol gave her another feeble smile. "It's a big house."

"Yeah," Veronica grumbled. "Too big. You ought to unload that place. It's got nothing but bad memories for you. What do you want to be clear out in the burbs for, anyway? It's like you're playing *Green Acres* or something."

"I am trying to sell it," Carol said with a shrug. "Nobody's buying, that's all."

"Humph," Veronica muttered skeptically.

Carol took a deep breath. "But what's funny, wherever the cat goes, he doesn't come back hungry. Both times I gave him fresh food. He just stared at me, then turned and walked away."

Veronica raised an eyebrow. "Wait. You're saying he was gone—inside the house—for a week, and when he showed up, he wasn't hungry? Baby, you must have a load of mice in your basement or worse. That cat's gotta be living on something."

Carol swallowed. "If I tell you something, will you promise not to think I'm crazy?"

Veronica raised her eyebrow higher. "Why would I think you're crazy? What's bothering you?"

Carol hesitated. Then she said, "My birthday was a little over a week ago. My aunt sent me flowers."

Veronica nodded for her to go on.

Carol squared her shoulders. "She's the only close relative I have left. But she doesn't get around much—she hates shopping—so she always has flowers sent. These were roses. Yellow roses. Baby ones."

"Okay," Veronica said. "So?"

Carol realized she'd been holding her breath. She let it out in a long, shuddering sigh.

"So the cat liked them. He doesn't seem to like much. But he kept jumping up on the table, rubbing against them. I almost think if he could purr, he would have."

She paused, remembering. "He almost tipped them over—and broke the stem on one. It wasn't really open yet. It was sort of a bud. So I pinched it off, and I tucked it under his collar.

"I said, 'Now you've got your flower. Keep out of mine.' And I put them up high, in a place he couldn't reach. An hour later he was gone, and he stayed gone for a whole week, like I said."

She fell silent, unwilling to say the rest.

"Has this story got a point?" Veronica asked.

Carol nodded. "When he came back, the flower was still in his collar. It was still fresh. The others were all dead by then. It was just opening."

Veronica's voice was disbelieving. "What are you telling me? He hid someplace in your house, and he came back with another flower?"

"It wasn't another flower. It was the same one. I recognized it. The way I'd pinched the stem off, at an angle. And it was still alive."

"Carol, stop. You're weirding me out. You imagined this."

Carol shook her head. "It happened. He was gone a week and the flower didn't die. It didn't change at all."

"Look at me," Veronica ordered.

Reluctantly, Carol met her friend's gaze.

Veronica leaned across the table, bringing her face close to Carol's. "That's it, baby," she said, concern in her voice. "You've been alone in that big house too long. You've got to get yourself a life. I mean it."

"Veronica," she protested, "I *didn't* imagine it. I don't know where he was, but while he was there, the rose didn't die."

"So where do you think he was?"

"I don't know."

Veronica leaned back against her chair, but she kept studying Carol's face solemnly. "I want you to come over to my house tonight. Have supper with Alvin and me."

"Veronica, it's not loneliness. I see people here all day long—"

"And," Veronica said with conviction, "if you don't like Charles, I'll tell you what I'll do. There's a new guy over in the law department. This weekend I'll invite you both for drinks. Have a couple of other people, make it really casual."

"I knew it," Carol said ruefully. "You think I've gone around the bend. I shouldn't have said anything."

"I don't think you've gone around the bend. But I think you're spending too much time dwelling on what's over, and you need to stop. You have to join the living again."

Join the living, Carol thought, stricken.

"Yes," Veronica said, kindly but firmly, "It's the truth. Give up the ghosts, Carol. Yes, honey. It's time."

CAROL LET Veronica affectionately bully her into having supper that night with her and Alvin. Veronica was an indifferent cook, but Alvin was a fine one and was presently going through a stir-fry phase.

"Give him a big enough wok and a place to stand," Veronica said, watching him, "and he'll stir-fry the world."

"My wok's plenty big enough to take care of you," Alvin said with a wink and a smile.

"I love your wok," Veronica said. "I don't have a complaint in the world about your wok. It keeps me satisfied."

Carol watched them fondly, but with a strange detachment, as if she were a visitor from another world observing a favorite pair of earthlings.

Alvin and Veronica loved each other in a quiet, companionable way. They were comfortable and easy together. And it was nice being with them. Not exciting, but very nice.

Yet try as she might, she was not able to imagine herself in the same sort of relationship with Charles, or, for that matter, anyone else. After Evan, such a life seemed beyond her comprehension.

When she went home to her empty house, however, it felt emptier than usual. Only the cat was there, and he did not welcome her. He lay on the couch and appeared to look straight through her, his green eyes half-closed.

She hung up her coat in the closet, sat down beside him and idly rubbed his silky black fur. He yawned in her face. The only other move he made was a twitch of his tail.

She'd had cats before, when she was growing up. She'd been an only child, born late in her parents' lives, and they'd let her keep pets so she wouldn't feel alone. But never had she known a cat as aloof, as unresponsive as Shadow.

His total silence made him seem even more otherworldly. She'd put a bell on his collar, but he managed to move so smoothly and stealthily that it seldom rang. It was like having a phantom cat, not a real one.

Perhaps, she thought in resignation, Veronica was right. She should get out of this house, mingle more, meet a man who could give her warmth and friendliness. She knew she would never find another great passion. But she might find affection, companionship, comfort.

Veronica claimed, with her usual frankness, that Carol was probably suffering from enormous sexual frustration. "You're young and healthy," Veronica had said. "It's a normal part of life. It's a *powerful* part. Now, you pretend it just doesn't exist? It won't work."

Alvin and Veronica had joked about finding her a man. "He doesn't have to make the earth move or bells ring," Veronica had said. "Just somebody nice and snuggly."

"We snuggly types," Alvin said, smiling, "are worth our weight in gold."

They'd insisted they'd have people in for drinks that weekend and ask the new man from the law department. Alvin said he would also invite a single man named Keats, who'd just been transferred to his firm from its St. Louis branch. A really nice, bright man, Alvin had said.

Carol tried to imagine meeting these faceless men, getting to know them, letting one of them touch her, kiss her. She tried to imagine herself in bed with a man again, not in wild passion, but just as Veronica said, in a nice, snuggly sort of way.

The cat's pale green eyes widened but looked cold, as if he were reading her mind and disapproved of what he saw. He edged away from her touch, rose and leaped from the couch. He landed so softly that the bell on his collar barely tinkled. Then he slipped around the corner and disappeared from sight.

"Shadow?" she said. "Kitty, kitty, kitty?"

She might as well have asked a real shadow to come at her bidding. He never came when he was called, and he was the only cat she'd ever encountered who wouldn't answer to "Kitty."

Resigned, she rose to go find him because she didn't want him disappearing again. But already he seemed to have vanished.

She stood at the foot of the rear stairs. The house had a double staircase, and he could have gone up either one. She checked the door to the basement. It was locked.

She sighed. She supposed he would reappear in his own good time, as usual. But where did he slip off to, so silently, and how did he hide himself so completely?

She did not allow herself to dwell on the mysterious rosebud. Veronica had convinced her that the flower had simply dried but had somehow retained the illusion of freshness.

When the cat did not reappear the next day, Carol forced herself not to worry about him. But he didn't return the day after that, or the one after that. It seemed as if she didn't actually have a cat.

"He's gone again," she told Veronica at coffee. "He walked around the corner into the hall Monday night, after I got back from your place, and he completely disappeared. I haven't seen him for three days."

"If that creepy cat was mine," Veronica said with feeling, "and he showed his creepy face again, I'd take him for a ride to the animal shelter. Why don't you get yourself a nice puppy or something?"

Carol didn't see the cat again until Saturday night. She had just come home from Alvin and Veronica's informal party. To her surprise, she'd had a good time and had laughed a good deal.

Bill Keats, the man from Alvin's office, was a squarely built, freckled man with hair as red as her own. He'd danced attendance on her, and she'd found it pleasant. When he'd asked for her phone number, she'd given it to him.

Mark Martinson, the new law professor, was more reserved, so cool he seemed almost illusive. He was handsome in a sleek, pale, Nordic way and acted like a careful man who was taking her measure.

But when she'd left, he made a point of leaving at the same time. He'd walked her to her car and asked her if she'd meet him for coffee or lunch sometime next week. She'd said she would like that just fine.

Now, as she took off her good coat and hung it in the hall closet, she thought that Veronica should be more than satisfied. She'd met two eligible men, and one of them, Bill Keats, seemed to be decidedly of the snuggly sort.

Then she turned on the stairwell light and started up to her bedroom, the smallest of the six. She was struck with surprise to see Shadow sitting on the top step, as silent and motionless as a cat carved of onyx.

Only his pale green eyes showed life as he lazily looked her up, then down. He appeared sleek and well fed. His black fur gleamed.

She sucked in her breath, rattled both by his inexplicable absence and his just-as-inexplicable reappearance. Then she realized something about him was different. His blue leather collar with the bell was gone. He wore a silver one in its place.

He watched her approach, then turned, as if bored, licked his paw and began to groom his whiskers. She reached the top stair and gazed at him in exasperation. "So, Mr. Mysterious, where were you this time?"

He ignored her and licked his paw again. She knelt to examine his silvery collar. "And what's this?" she demanded. "You really must be getting out of the house somehow. You have a new wardrobe, and it's certainly not from me."

She stared at the silver links and found, suddenly, that she couldn't breathe. Her heart began to pound madly, and tears sprang, burning, to her eyes. "No," she whispered in shock. "Oh, no. No."

The cat eyed her steadily, seeming, as usual, to see through her. Her hands shaking, she reached out and unfastened the chain from his neck. It fell into her palm, still warm from his body.

It was a man's identification bracelet, sterling silver. On the nameplate was engraved Dr. Evan J. Glendower. On the reverse side were the words "To Evan—Love Is Eternal—Always, Carol."

She sat numbly on the top stair, turning the nameplate over and over, reading it again and again. This *was* her wedding gift to Evan, the very bracelet. She recognized the long, curved scratch just beneath his name; he had done that on the trip to Tanzania.

Evan had been wearing this bracelet when he died, and Dr. Sales had sworn it was on his wrist when his body was cremated. Like Evan's body, it had been fired into near nothingness and scattered over the waters of the Slave Coast.

This was a bracelet that no longer existed. But it was solid and real and heavy in her hand.

2

SHE SAT stunned and trembling. Beside her, the cat calmly licked his paw again, then began to groom its pointed ears.

She unclenched her fist and stared once more at the bracelet. It was Evan's—she had no doubt. But she was told it had been destroyed in Africa. How could it appear on the neck of a cat in Illinois?

She tried to stop shaking, but couldn't. The thick silver links brought back memories so sharp they hurt, twisting like a knife in her stomach.

Evan's brown wrist, dusted with golden brown hairs that glinted bright in the Nigerian sun. The bracelet shining against his skin. The small white scar, shaped like a hook, at the base of one knuckle. The warm feel of his hand on her nape.

Evan's blue eyes looking into hers, intent with desire. The darkness of his lashes, his sun-streaked, wavy hair, bronzed face. His lips, slightly parted, lowering to take hers . . .

The cat rose, stretched languidly, then turned, creeping down the dim hallway. In a moment he would disappear into the shadows.

No, you don't, Carol thought, half in panic, half in anger. Not again. Clutching the bracelet more tightly still, she sprang to her feet and switched on the hall light.

Her knees felt weak, but she steeled herself to follow the cat. Soundlessly he rounded a corner and slipped from sight. She hurried after him, her heart beating hard.

He stood motionless for a second in the center of the dim hall, not looking back at her. Then he stole up the two steps that led to the locked tower bedroom. Her breath caught in her throat, a tight, choking feeling.

Shadow rubbed against the closed door almost sensually. It eased open just slightly. Without hesitation, he slipped inside, disappearing into the room's darkness.

No, she thought again, dazed. He couldn't do that. The door was locked, the key gone.

But she forced herself to follow, even though she hadn't been inside the octagonal bedroom for more than a year. She pushed the door open and fumbled for the light switch. The bulbs in the overhead fixture blazed to life, illuminating the room.

The cat had leaped onto the large raised platform that supported the antique bed. He cast her the briefest of glances; his pupils slitted against the sudden light made his eyes almost totally green. Then he slipped beneath the bed and disappeared.

She stood staring after him, her heart thudding in her chest. *He can't have gotten into this room—it's locked,* she thought. *He couldn't have had this bracelet—it's gone.*

She looked down again at the ID bracelet. She'd gripped it so hard that her fingernails had cut small, raw crescents into her palm. They stung and oozed blood.

Against all reason, the bracelet still lay gleaming and heavy in her hand. Its silver was lightly flecked on the nameplate by her own blood.

All right, she told herself, *there's a rational explanation for this. There has to be.* But she felt faint and frightened, and her heart thundered in her chest.

The tower door should be locked. She'd thrown the key away more than a year ago. But the door was open.

You're a scientist. Think logically, she ordered herself.

The house was for sale. The real estate agent had asked her about the locked bedroom once. She'd told him she kept it shut and had lost the key.

"I can't show a locked room," he'd said. "You'll have to call a locksmith and have a new key made."

She'd tossed her head rather haughtily. She hadn't chosen to explain herself. It was too painful.

"I can't be bothered," she'd said. "You have one made if you want. I don't use the room."

He'd stared at her as if realizing suddenly that she was odd. She didn't care. "I don't use it," she repeated. "If you open it, be sure you lock it again. I don't want it open."

He'd nodded and said nothing. But he'd kept giving her that nervous, searching look. Later he'd tried to set a time with her for a locksmith to come.

"I don't want to know anything about it," she said. "Do it while I'm at the university. You know my hours."

Now she pushed her hand tensely through her hair. Of course. The real estate agent must have had a new key made. It was simple. Of course.

Relieved, she still felt her pulse leaping in her throat. She didn't even know how many times the house had been shown or when. Her orders were to show it only in her absence.

At the end of every visit, a sales agent left a business card on her kitchen counter, and there was a sizable and untidy heap of these cards. She never kept track of them or noticed when a new one was added.

She began to breathe more easily. Of course. Someone had shown the house and accidentally left the room unlocked—that was all.

Feeling drained, she leaned against the doorframe and, for the first time in sixteen months, looked around the room. It seemed larger and barer than she'd remembered.

Tattered shades blinded the windows, which were bare of curtains. A dry, dusty scent lay upon the air. The wallpaper, yellowing and striped with dulled silver, hung in strips in places.

The enormous bed was the only piece of furniture in the room. That and an abandoned full-length mirror that was losing its silver. The mirror, its mahogany frame cracked and chipped, leaned against the far wall.

She looked at her image, dim in the lusterless glass. A small, pale woman stared back at her. Her tousled hair seemed an incongruously cheerful color, the warm red gold of fire.

She lowered her gaze to the bracelet again. She could explain how the tower bedroom was unlocked. But what of this, the silver links and nameplate in her bloodied hand?

I misunderstood, she told herself. *Dr. Sales must have said one thing and done another. He sent me the bracelet. I was in shock. I put it away. I forgot it because I wanted to forget.*

She nodded numbly. Or perhaps even she'd only imagined that Sales had said the bracelet would stay with the body. She'd been in such a terrible state when Evan died she might have misunderstood anything, blocked any memory, made up any sort of fiction to comfort herself.

Yes, said the scientist in her. But how did the bracelet get on the cat? And where did his collar go?

Perhaps the bracelet had been returned to her and she'd hidden it somewhere, unable to bear looking at it. She'd tucked it away in some nook or cranny, denying to herself that it even existed.

Somehow the cat had lost its collar and managed to get the cast-off bracelet around its neck. Oh, God, no, that was a perfectly ridiculous scenario, unbelievable. She could never believe such a coincidence.

A chilling thought struck her. Had *she* put the bracelet on the cat's neck? Was she having spells of amnesia or some other sort of mental aberration?

The room's eight bare walls seemed to close in on her; the antique bed loomed, too large and too empty. *We would have made love in that bed,* she thought. *We would have conceived our children there.*

She wanted out of the damned, mocking room. She never wanted to look into it again. And she wanted Shadow to keep out of it, as well. He was trespassing, violating the place.

"Come out here," she commanded the unseen cat. "I mean it. Get out here."

Of course he did not appear, and nothing answered her except silence. The bed was covered carelessly with an enormous fringed throw. Its worn folds fell to the floor, the faded pattern no longer discernible.

"Damned cat," Carol said resentfully. She stepped onto the dais, knelt beside the bed. "Come out," she demanded even more sternly.

The throw did not so much as quiver. The room was so quiet she could hear her blood drum in her ears.

"All right," she said between clenched teeth. "If you won't come out, I'll drag you out, you demon."

She transferred the bracelet to her left hand so that she could reach beneath the bed with her right. It would be undignified, groping beneath the bed for the hiding cat, but she was too aggravated to care. With her left hand, she lifted the fringed throw.

Her fingers tingled oddly. It was as if a sudden electrical shock rippled through them. A strange bluish glow seemed to spill from beneath the fringe, as though a theater curtain had risen to reveal a ghostly light.

Now, she thought in agitation, *my eyes are playing tricks.* She ignored the illusion and stretched her hand beneath the bed.

She looked under the bed for the cat so that she could seize him by the scruff and pull him back into the open. Nothing could have prepared her for what she saw.

There was nothing under the bed except an infinity of space filled with eerie blue light. She could see no end to the still blue light. She could see no cat. She could not see her hand.

She gasped and snatched her hand back. It reappeared, as if by magic. But beneath the bed, the azure light seemed to stretch forever.

Once again she could not get her breath, and a weight seemed to oppress her chest. She was filled with horror, yet wonder, too. She could not stop staring into the luminous infinity.

It did not shimmer; it did not change color. It had almost a solidity to it, a thick, static haziness that teased the sight and confounded the brain.

I'm dreaming, she told herself. *This is all right, because I'm only dreaming.*

But the light seemed real enough to be palpable. Carefully she reached into it. Once again her hand disappeared, swallowed by the steady blue light.

She snatched it back and it was restored to her, visible once more and appearing normal, but full of strange tingling. She gazed at it in disbelief and flexed her fingers.

She was too stunned to move away. She was not sure she *could* move. Her body seemed peculiarly heavy, as if some force pinioned her.

For the third time she thrust her hand into the light, deeper this time, halfway to her elbow. She felt nothing, but her hand quite simply vanished. It appeared to have merged with the solid light.

She drew it back more slowly, toying with the light. She could make her fingertips disappear all at once or one at a time, like a conjuring trick. There was no effect except the tingle, which was beginning to feel almost pleasant.

The more closely she stared at the blue glow, the deeper it seemed. It was as if she were poised at the edge of a new universe, some unexpected and further reach of reality.

She could extend her hand upward, far past where the bed should have cut off her reach. She could lower it as far as she dared. There was no floor beneath the bed. There was nothing but the limitless azure light.

Then, from far away, from an infinitely long distance, she heard a plaintive sound. It was the mew of a cat. It sounded lonely, as if it wanted and needed her.

She froze. She heard the cat's yearning cry again.

Shadow, she thought, her fear rushing back. He was there, somehow hidden in the midst of the light. And he wanted her to come to him.

But Shadow had no cry. He never made sounds. Not ever. Yet the mew echoed again, as if calling to her, pleading for her to come.

My God, he wants me in there, she thought in suddenly rising terror. *He's trying to get me to come in there with him.*

She snatched her hand away from the pleasant, beckoning light. She let the fringed throw fall back to the floor, cutting off any glimpse of the shining. She sat up and looked once more in disbelief at Evan's bracelet.

Her left hand was cramped from clutching it so possessively. She transferred it to her right hand and stared for the hundredth time at his name engraved deep in the silver, at the familiar scratch.

Then she found herself gazing at her hand, the one that had been in the light. It was no longer bloody, but clean. The cuts were healed.

"Oh, my God," she said, fighting a feeling of faintness.

What was happening to her? The wounds had been real. She'd seen them, known their pain, felt the stickiness of her blood.

She hadn't imagined the cuts on her palm; she was certain. No more than she imagined the heavy bracelet, which she still could not explain.

And the cat, which is mute, is calling for me to come to him. Under my bed is some kind of alternate universe. And I'm going insane.

She stumbled to her feet and realized that tears streaked her face. She made her way to the door, switched off the bedroom light and slammed the door behind her. She slammed it hard, so that the cat couldn't open it.

In panic, she fled downstairs. She nearly stumbled on the stairs, but she managed to get to the first floor. She turned on all the lights.

Blindly she made her way across the kitchen, accidentally knocking over a chair. She didn't bother to right it. She'd hurt her shin against one of the rungs, but she hardly felt the pain.

She fumbled through the heap of cards the real estate agents had left on the counter, but they told her nothing. Putting her hands to her temples, she tried to think. She should call someone: Veronica, Charles, somebody, anybody.

She reached for the phone, not caring how late it was. But then she heard the faintest of sounds, and she froze, her finger poised over the phone's buttons. Moving like a shadow, the black cat came through the kitchen door.

His brass bell tinkled faintly. His blue collar was securely in place, as if it had never been gone. And the silver identification bracelet was still in her hand.

SHE ENDED UP not calling anyone. She shut the cat in the kitchen and slept on the living room couch with all the lights turned on. At first she dozed uneasily, but at last she sank into deeper sleep.

She dreamed of Evan so vividly that it seemed she had traveled back in time. It was as if she were actually *with* him again. In astonishing detail, she relived one hot Sunday night in their apartment in Ibadan.

She'd come back from a weekend trip to the western Sudan. She'd been sent with a Nigerian nurse and a woman doctor in a special contingent to deal with the notoriously shy women of the Lassa Ubi tribe.

They'd gone to gather blood samples. It was January, the dry season, which brought the yearly outbreak of lethal meningitis in the Lassa area. Specimens needed to be drawn, brought back to Ibadan for study.

The Sudan was hellish in January. Acrid dust the color of dried blood filled the windy air. The sun baked the air and earth, until the heat rose above one hundred and twenty degrees.

She'd returned home sunburned and dirty. She had dust in every pore, she told Evan. She could feel it grinding between her teeth, taste its bitterness in the back of her throat.

He made her brush her teeth five times with bottled water. He had a cool bath ready for her (the apartment had no shower) and, luxury of luxuries, American shampoo and bubble bath.

He stripped her filthy clothes from her and helped her, laughing, get into the tub. He scrubbed her down, alternating between a bath brush, a loofah and a thick washcloth. It was bliss to be with him, to be touched all over and caressed by him.

"Maybe we missed a spot here," he said in her ear as he soaped her breasts. He kissed her nape.

"Or here," he whispered, his hand moving below the bubbles.

His touch lulled her and made her languid. At the same time he aroused and excited her.

Calmly, deliberately, he used his hands and mouth to make her faint with desire. Then, when she was almost dissolving with yearning, he helped her from the cool bath and wrapped her in a large white towel.

He kissed the back of her neck again. "I've got champagne chilling," he said against her damp hair.

"I don't want champagne," she said, turning to him. She let the towel fall away and wound her arms around his neck. "I want you," she said, straining against him.

He kissed her, his tongue moving sensually about hers, over and under, sometimes letting only the tip tease her sensitive inner lip. She moved her hands to his shirt, unbuttoned it blindly. She gasped and lay her cheek against the muscled warmth of his chest, listening to the hard beat of his heart.

He held her close, his arousal pressed against her. He kissed her damp throat, her shoulders. His hands moved down her naked body slowly, possessively.

"I don't want you in the Sudan again," he said in her ear, his voice tight. "I worried about you the whole time."

"It's the only time I've ever been," she said, her lips against his chest. "I had to. For the women. You've gone off. You'll go again."

"That's different," he said. "Something might happen to you. I couldn't stand it. I won't let them send you again."

She slid her hands up beneath his shirt to his bare shoulders. She pressed her mouth to the hollow of his throat. His skin tasted clean and warm and slightly salty.

"What about you?" she murmured. "What if something happened to you?"

"Nothing's going to happen to me," he vowed. "I love you too much. I'll always come back to you. Always."

"Promise?" she said, kissing his throat.

"Promise," he said. "No matter what."

She could feel the vital power in his shoulders beneath her fingertips. His breath gently fanned her hair, her ear, her moist throat. His arms were strong around her.

He's there, he's real. She could sense it all—his scent; the soft, tense sound of his breathing; the taste of him; the sight of his tall, beautiful body; the feel of him against her. *Yes, this is real. I'm with him, with him. I love you, Evan.*

But the dream veered off into vagueness, and Evan grew dimmer and more distant; he disappeared. Hard as she struggled to get back to him, she stayed lost in empty darkness. She could not even find the dream of him.

She awoke, frustrated, aching from the hard couch and not truly rested. But she did feel strangely and coolly *sane.* Somehow Evan had done that. It was as if he had come to her in her sleep to comfort her and keep her strong.

Events of the night before no longer seemed real. They seemed far more dreamlike than her dream of Evan. They were will-o'-the-wisps, illusory and quickly fading.

But there was one disturbing fact. She had Evan's ID bracelet. It must have been in her possession all along, she told herself. The cat had not brought it to her. The cat had nothing to do with it. Shadow, although aloof, was only an ordinary animal. She went to the kitchen and quietly opened the door to check on him. He was taking a nap on his rag rug in the corner, oblivious to the world.

She closed the door again, reassured. She must have been thrown into shock by rediscovering the forgotten bracelet. It had caused her to imagine things—or given her a particularly intense nightmare.

She felt the urge to talk to someone sensible, like Veronica, or even merely dully dependable, like Charles. But it was too early to phone anyone in Chicago.

It was not, however, too early to call Nigeria. It was past noon in Nigeria. With luck, Dr. Akinyere Sales would be home from church.

He would tell her that he had sent the bracelet back. Then she would piece together what she had done with it and how she had taken possession of it again last night. She would work out a logical explanation.

She got out her phone and address book, her heart doing a queer, unhappy dance in her chest. She had not talked to Sales since Evan's death. She had not had the courage.

It took a long time to make the connection to Ibadan. But then the number rang, and she heard Sales's voice, courtly and dignified, greeting her in his native Hausan language.

"Dr. Sales," she said in English. "This is Carol Glendower in Chicago. I hope I'm not interrupting you."

He switched to his lilting English. "Oh, Professor Glendower. It is a delight to hear from you. You are well, I hope."

"Perfectly fine," she lied. "And you? And your family?"

"We are all most fine. Your work, it goes well?"

She made appropriate small talk, gave him the right answers, asked the right questions. Her lucidity reassured her. No hallucinating madwoman would carry on such a rational, civil conversation.

Politely she worked her way to the reason for her call. "I want you to refresh my memory," she said. "When Evan—when Dr. Glendower died, I went through a bad patch. There are things that simply never registered on my mind, I'm afraid."

"Great grief can work mischief on the memory, I fear," Dr. Sales said gallantly. "What is it you wish to know?"

She hesitated. She could envision Dr. Akinyere Sales clearly: tall, dark and professorial, with his perfect manners and horn-rimmed glasses. He had a Nigerian's innate courtesy and was a man of scrupulous honesty.

"It's a small matter," she said. "It's about his identification bracelet. You were the one who sent it back to me, weren't you? I don't think I ever thanked you."

It was Sales's turn to pause. "Oh, no," he said in his deep voice. "He was *most* insistent. He kept the bracelet with him. Oh, no, no. He would not be parted from it, not even in death. And this is how it was."

His words seemed to knock the air from her lungs. For safekeeping, she had fastened the bracelet around her wrist. She stared at it, touched it to assure herself it was real.

"I...think there's some mistake," she said weakly. "The bracelet was returned to me. I have it now."

But Dr. Sales was insistent. He sounded wounded, almost indignant. "I am sorry, Professor Glendower. That is not possible. Sister Mary Sarah at the hospital will tell you the same thing. The bracelet was still with him at the end. We both saw to that. We had promised him."

"Oh," she said, feeling more breathless than before.

"We were worried that it might be stolen," Sales persisted. "It was his wish that it stay with him. We were honor-bound to grant it. It was done."

Carol's breathlessness made her throat ache and her head swim.

Sales went on, conviction in his voice. "We saw it. A few blackened lumps of metal with the ash. She and I and Pastor Nigel. We all saw. Pastor Nigel and I scattered the ashes ourselves. I saw it all, ash and silver, sink beneath the waves. He will tell you exactly the same."

"I'm sorry—terribly, terribly sorry," she apologized. "As I say, my mind wasn't clear at the time. I've mistaken it with another piece of his jewelry. Forgive me. I trust you absolutely."

She prayed she had not hurt Dr. Sales by appearing to doubt his honesty. She *did* trust him absolutely.

As for Sister Mary Sarah, Carol clearly remembered her. She was a no-nonsense woman, as conscientious as a saint. Evan used to joke he could see the beginnings of a halo around her head.

And Pastor Nigel? He was a stern, punctilious man, intolerant of wrongdoing in himself or others. She could not ask for three more reliable witnesses.

When she hung up, the ghost of last night's fear returned, haunting her again. All right, she told herself nervously. The real bracelet had been destroyed.

Sometime in the first haze of her sorrow, she must have had another one made. It was a foolish, romantic gesture, but she must have done it, then forgotten. Stricken with wanting Evan, she must have even duplicated the scratch on the bracelet.

She sat down on the edge of the couch and put her forehead in her hand.

I grieved for him more than I knew, she thought. *Losing him made me a little crazy for a while. I didn't know what I was doing.*

That was it, she told herself wearily. And she was still grieving. Last night she'd thought of going out with other men, of being in bed with another man, and guilt had temporarily shaken her into irrationality.

So she'd looked at the bracelet, and in her fevered emotions, she'd imagined things or dreamed them. Guilt and sorrow had temporarily twisted her thought processes.

She still loved Evan too much to think of anyone else. And guilt had punished her for even trying.

She sighed and rose to make herself coffee. She was a scientist. She lived in a world governed by laws and logic. There were reasons, medical or psychological, for what had happened to her.

She would discover those reasons. Her unruly emotions would be dealt with rationally, and she would not be ruled by them.

But all morning long, she thought uneasily about the tower bedroom. She should go back. Enter it and look under the bed and prove to herself there was nothing there.

She would see nothing harmful or supernatural. Then she could laugh at her own foolishness.

Yes, it was the simplest answer. Go look again, in the cold light of day.

That would be the end of it.

But she could not make herself do it.

3

THAT NIGHT she dreamed of Evan again. There was no fantasy in the dream; it mirrored past events exactly and so vividly it was as if she were living them again. She was in Nigeria, Evan was with her and life was good.

Evan had wanted to go north to the village of Bida to meet a British entymologist, but he didn't want to leave her. She'd gone with him to the highland savanna, where they had stayed at the Government Catering Rest House.

Their white bungalow had a tiled floor and freshly whitewashed walls. A creaking ceiling fan stirred the air, and instead of one bed, there were two, spartan and narrow.

Layers of mosquito netting swathed both beds, which made them resemble traps, not places to rest. Carol looked at them in dismay because she didn't want to sleep apart from Evan. But he gave her a teasing smile and arched an eyebrow wickedly.

"What do you think?" he asked. "My place or yours?"

She pretended not to be interested, just to tease him back. "Neither. I'll keep to myself tonight. You brought me all this way to talk to a man about rat fleas."

The Englishman had been a mine of almost too much information. At supper, the more of the strong Nigerian beer he drank, the more he droned on about his favorite subject: the rat flea.

"Hey," Evan said, catching her around the waist. He pulled her to him, her back against his chest. "Do I know how to show a girl a good time, or what?"

"Or what, I think," she said with false aloofness, but he was kissing her behind the ear, making her shuddery and restless with yearning.

"You were very good," he said, his lips moving to her throat. "You only yawned twice."

"I was a marvel of restraint," she said. She couldn't pretend any longer. She leaned her head back against his shoulder and closed her eyes as his hands moved under her blue cambric shirt.

"The time for restraint is over," he said softly.

He caressed the smooth skin of her stomach and drew her closer, so that her hips rested against his groin. She could feel his growing hardness.

His hands rose to her breasts, which tautened at his caress. His fingers traced slow circles around her nipples, tempting and tantalizing her.

"Unbutton your blouse," he said, his lips against her ear.

With trembling hands she undid the buttons.

"Now," he said, kissing the curve of her shoulder, "undo your bra."

The bra fastened in front. Her fingers brushed his as she unsnapped it. Then her breasts were free and bare, and he touched her as only he could do.

When she turned to undo his shirt, his beautiful blue eyes were languorous with desire. In the light of the single lamp, his skin was bronze and his thick brown hair glinted with gold.

He shrugged out of his shirt, letting it fall to the floor. Then he slowly drew her shirt down off her shoulders, as if unveiling her. He bent and kissed her on each throbbing breast.

Every time Evan made love to her, it was as if he seduced her anew. He explored her body expertly, finding her most sensitive points, making her burn and tremble with desire.

Sometimes he aroused her so much that she thought she would dissolve with wanting him. It pleased her greatly that she exerted the same power over him. Together they made sex into an intoxicating art.

She knew this was possible only because they loved each other so completely. Sexually, they kept discovering new frontiers. They made love in different ways, with wildness or quiet tenderness, reverence or irreverence, seriously or playfully.

They laughed that night in Bida. It took great acrobatic doing to have sex on the narrow, unsteady bed and not bring down the mosquito netting on top of them.

Afterward, as cramped and uncomfortable as the bed was, Carol had refused to go to the lonely other bed, and Evan didn't want her to. They didn't sleep well, but at least they slept together.

She lay with her face pressed against his chest, her cheek tickled by his crisp chest hair. He had one bare arm around her, holding her to him. She could nestle against the whole length of his body. His breath stirred her hair, and she could hear the beat of his heart.

SLOWLY, reluctant to leave her dreams, she awoke. She turned in her bed to touch Evan. She wanted to lay her hand on his biceps, then snuggle against his warmth, to nuzzle him sleepily. . .

But he was not there. Her eyes fluttered open, and all she saw was darkness. Evan was gone. His heart had stopped, his breath had ceased and his beautiful body was ashes.

She touched the silver identification bracelet on her wrist, then pressed her face against the pillow and wept. She cried until she could cry no more.

When at last she rose, the Chicago morning was iron gray and snow was falling. Looking about the house, she was shaken to realize that Shadow had once again vanished. She tried not to think of the mysterious cat or the tower bedroom.

Forcing herself to be cool and efficient, she made ready for the day. She kept the bracelet on her wrist, hidden beneath the sleeve of her bulky sweater.

At school she made one phone call from her office, to schedule a doctor's appointment for that afternoon. Then she went to teach her morning class. The class went well, yet she felt peculiarly distant from the students, even from herself, as if they were all characters in a not-very-interesting play.

Afterward she met Veronica for a quick coffee. Carol tried to act as normal as possible. She did not speak of the bracelet or the cat or the tower bedroom or the blue light.

Instead she said she'd had a fine time Saturday night, just wonderful.

"So. Are you going to break down and see either one of those men again?" Veronica challenged.

Smiling, Carol said she just might see them both.

"Good," Veronica said with exaggerated relief. "Then I have not lived in vain."

When Carol got back to her office, she found a note asking her to phone Mark Martinson in the law department. She did, and he asked her to have lunch at the campus pub. But during lunch, although she smiled and said all the right things, she felt as if she were an android.

Mark asked her to go to a play the following Friday. She said she'd love to. In truth she realized she didn't find him attractive after all. He was too contained and studied, and there was something calculating in his pale eyes.

She went back to the biology department and taught her afternoon class. It, too, went well, but again she had the eerie feeling of watching events from a great distance.

Then she canceled her office hour and drove to a medical complex in the suburbs, far from the university. Christmas was only three weeks away, and the decorated tree in the clinic's entrance seemed to mock her. For the first time in her life, she was consulting a psychiatrist, and now that she was there, she was frightened.

DR. JERRY BRATLING was a lean, homely man with a bushy head of hair and thick glasses. Carol knew him from her graduate school days. He and his girlfriend, Carmen, had lived in the next-door apartment; the three of them had been impoverished students together.

They'd shared suppers of meat loaf or macaroni and the occasional luxury of a six-pack. They'd also shared all the triumphs and woes of student life and had developed a strong sense of comradeship.

Now Carmen was Jerry's wife, and they were expecting their second child. Carol had stayed in touch, but she had never imagined she'd come to Jerry as a patient. He had been extraordinarily kind to work her into his schedule on such short notice.

He didn't make her lie on a couch or ask about her infancy and potty training. He sat across from her, listening to her story quietly, showing no emotion, offering no judgments.

At last he said, "And what do you make of all this?" He took off his glasses and calmly polished them.

Carol sucked in her breath. A nervous ache beat in the pit of her stomach. "I *think* I know what happened," she said carefully.

He gave her a nearsighted glance. "Yes?"

"When Evan died, I was in shock. There are things I simply can't remember. It's like my memory's a slate and part of it's wiped clean."

He nodded. "Depression affects memory. Some people don't know that."

She gripped the smooth leather arms of her chair more tightly. "I think that I must have gone to a jeweler and had another bracelet made. As a way of hanging on to Evan. I must have even scratched it, so it'd really seem like his."

"And?"

Her stomach hurt harder. "And . . . I must have put the bracelet away, then blocked it from my mind. Because it brought him back too clearly, and I miss him too much."

Jerry put his glasses back on and gazed at her mildly. "So why do you think the bracelet surfaced again now?"

She pushed up her sweater sleeve, put her hand over the ID almost protectively. "I was thinking about being unfaithful to him. I—I'd been thinking maybe I should have an affair."

Jerry scratched his jaw meditatively. "It's interesting you used the term 'unfaithful.'"

"Well, it's how I feel. I'm not ready for some casual little fling. Maybe I'll never be ready."

"And what does that feeling have to do with the bracelet reappearing, Carol?"

She paused, struggling to sound as rational as possible. "Two men at a party the other night said they'd like to see me again. I think that on a conscious level I encouraged them. But on a deeper level, I resisted. So I went home, and I dug out the bracelet. . . ."

"The idea of being 'unfaithful' made you bring it out?"

"Yes," she said earnestly. "As if to rebuke myself for what I was thinking. To remind me of what I'd lost."

He lifted one eyebrow thoughtfully. "But you don't actually remember taking the bracelet out again?"

"No," she admitted. "Perhaps I was so upset deep down that I did it unconsciously. I have no memory of doing it."

His expression stayed neutral. "But you do have a memory of the cat sitting on the stairs? And that the bracelet was on his neck?"

"I *seem* to have that memory," she said, shaking her head. "Maybe seeing the bracelet again gave me such a shock that I—I fell into a waking nightmare."

She looked at him searchingly. "A professor once told me that. That you can have a nightmare while you're wide awake. She said hers was about yellow spiders. That it felt totally real to her."

Jerry smiled slightly. "Quite normal people can have hallucinations under certain conditions. Including great emotional stress."

She sank back against the chair, relieved. "So you think my explanation makes sense?"

He smiled again. "Carol, you always have been the most maddeningly logical woman I've ever met. If all my patients could analyze their experiences the way you can, I'd be out of business."

"But why such a bizarre scenario?" she asked. "The cat, the bedroom, that—that strange space under the bed full of blue light?"

"Let me be frank. And Freudian. All these things have sexual connotations. The cat can symbolize female sexuality. The cat with the ID for a collar shows you still believe your sexuality belongs to your late husband."

"I see," she said, her cheeks warming slightly.

"The tower," Jerry said with a wry face, "well, old Freud would have fun with that. Male sex symbol. You've kept the tower inaccessible. You've locked it away."

Carol blushed a bit more hotly, but nodded.

"As for looking under the bed," Jerry said, his eyes twinkling, "that's the classic action of the spinster, right? And what's she looking for?"

"A man," Carol said, resisting the desire to wriggle with discomfort.

"Exactly," he said with a kind smile. "Symbolically, you followed your sexuality to the bed, the place where sex takes place. But when you looked beneath it, as if for a partner, all you allowed yourself to see was emptiness. Emptiness forever. And it was blue. Blue symbolizes sadness."

Her mind spun. "What about my hand? How I hurt my hand and then the light seemed to heal it?"

"You gave your hand in marriage," Jerry said sagely. "When you lost your husband it was like a wound. Your grief says the only thing that will ease the wound is a life of emptiness."

"All that symbolism was in this—this hallucination?"

"I'd say so," he told her. "Early in your grieving process, you had what we call fugue states. Periods in which you forget what you did. Such as getting the bracelet reproduced."

"I see," she said, but it troubled her that her mind, so rational and orderly before Evan's death, should have sprung so many tricks, twists and turns on her.

"And," Jerry went on, "when you contemplated starting a new sexual relationship, your grief threw you into another short fugue, in which you retrieved the bracelet. At the sight of it, your mind created a little drama in which your conflicts were stylized and symbolized so you could face them."

"Well," she said, embarrassed, "the whole thing was upsetting. More than upsetting. Terrifying, really. What do I do now?"

His smile faded, but his expression was kind. "You've done exactly the right thing in coming to talk about it. It's what I'd expect from a woman of your intelligence. As for your next step . . ."

"Yes?" she said expectantly.

"I think maybe you *should* get involved with another man. Not plunge in blindly. That's not your style. But find yourself a wholesome and healing relationship."

She hadn't wanted to hear that advice. She clasped the bracelet more possessively. "But I'm not ready. That's what this whole thing is telling me."

He sighed. He reached over and gave her hand a brotherly pat. "What this whole thing is telling you," he said, "is that it's time to let go of the past. For your own emotional health, it's time to get on with your life."

"Are you telling me this as a doctor or as my friend?" she asked defensively.

"As both," he said. "And maybe you should come talk to me a few more times. Just to help you through the transition."

The transition, she thought, suddenly feeling trapped. *Into accepting a world without Evan. I don't want that transition.*

Her feelings must have shown on her face.

"Carol," he said, "I see that stubborn set to your chin. But what's over is over. You've got to come to terms."

She looked at his homely, friendly, concerned face. A lump rose in her throat. "I know that," she said tightly.

He nodded in encouragement. "And Carol? Another thing."

"Yes?" she said apprehensively.

He paused a moment. "I'd get rid of that bracelet," he advised. "Don't wear it. Put it away again."

The knot in her throat grew more painful. She said, "I know."

But her heart rebelled. She didn't want to take off the bracelet. Not now. Not ever.

IT WAS SNOWING HARDER as she drove home.

Jerry had reassured her and given her back her faith in her sanity. Yet she was troubled. Although his intricate explanation of the symbolism of the incident made sense, it seemed too pat, too easy.

She'd asked him about her peculiar dreams. Why were they so realistic? Why did she feel she was back in Africa, experiencing events with Evan as if for the first time?

Jerry had tried to set her at ease about that, too. "The mind is an amazing thing, Carol. It can make reality seem like a dream and vice versa."

He'd patted her hand again. "You haven't made it through the acceptance stage of your grief. The dreams are a form of denial. Now you can start putting denial aside, get on with the healing process."

What healing process? she'd thought bitterly. There was no "healing" for the loss of Evan. The only way she would be healed would be to have him back again, and that was impossible.

Lately, instead of her memories of him fading, they had grown stronger and more vivid. She remembered the long weekend they had spent at the luxury resort on Golwanda Beach. It had been their eighth-month anniversary, and the stay had been his present to her.

The long stretch of flawless beach had sparkled whitely in the sun. The blue waves came tumbling in with a low, rhythmic thunder that seemed to get into her pulses.

She and Evan had been lying on the beach, he reading, she stretched out beside him on her stomach, staring dreamily at the surf. Then Evan had put down his book and peered at her with scientific interest.

"That sun's getting high," he said. "I should baste you again."

He sat up, took the bottle of coconut suntan lotion and straddled her body at the thighs. He began slowly to massage the oil onto her shoulders, upper arms, her back. His hands moved hypnotically to the beat of the waves.

"Umm," Carol said, and stretched luxuriously. "That's wonderful. Don't ever stop."

She felt the muscularity and heat of his bare thighs imprisoning hers. His hands roamed over her with beguiling sensuality. They moved to the back of her waist. His thumbs kneaded her spine, making her feel languid and tingly.

"You're getting a brand-new crop of freckles," he said. "I'll count 'em tonight. And kiss the new ones hello." He bent and kissed the back of her neck, a lingering, teasing kiss.

"I wish I had the nerve to take my top off," she said when he straightened up and started stroking her again, "and get freckled all over."

"Nope," he said firmly. "You get enough kisses there already. And I don't want those pretty treasures burned."

She smiled.

"Hmm," he said. "Now, how do I get the backs of your legs done? Without moving. I'm starting to enjoy this position."

"I'm aware of that." She sighed happily. "I feel ample evidence."

"If it gets any more ample, I'll be arrested. I'd better move."

With a slight groan, he swung his leg from her and sat beside her, instead. He rubbed the lotion up and down her thighs, her calves, stroking with provocative deliberation.

She turned to him and took the bottle of lotion. "Now I'll do you."

His smile was white and wicked. "You'll do me? I like the sound of that."

"Satyr," she teased. She poured the warm lotion into her hand and began to work the liquid onto his shoulders.

He had big shoulders, broad, powerful and sun bronzed. He looked gorgeous to her with the blue sea and sky behind him like a perfect backdrop.

The past two days had streaked his brown hair with more gold, giving him a slightly leonine look. He wore only three things—his silver ID, his wedding ring and a very small black bathing suit.

The sun had gilded his hard body and limbs so that he resembled a pagan god, she thought. The sea wind tousled his hair, and the tang of the spray mingled with the scent of coconut oil.

His eyes were of the same vivid blue as the sky, and they were trained on her.

"Yep," he said softly. "You've got a million new freckles. And I'll have to kiss them all."

She glanced in dismay at her arms. "I'm more polkadotted than I've ever been in my life. I wish I could tan like you."

"No," he said, studying the constellation of freckles in the valley between her breasts. "I like you exactly the way you are. I like all your places that are polka-dotted. And your places that aren't."

"Turn," she said, "so I can do your back."

"If I turn, I can't see you," he said. "I want to memorize the way you are today. I'll go back to that memory a lot. Especially while we're apart."

Her spirits, playful and erotic a moment before, suddenly sank. She took off her sunglasses and stared at him, as if she must memorize his face, too. In seven weeks she must go back to the States.

"How can I stand it?" she asked, fighting back the urge to cry. "Being apart from you for two whole months?"

"We won't be apart," he said, becoming serious. "It's not possible for me to be apart from you. You'll be with me all the time. Here." He touched his bare chest, over his heart.

She put her hand on his and held it there. She could feel the strong, steady beat of his heart. Her own pounded painfully.

"You'll be with me, too," she said softly. "Here." She pressed her fingertips between her breasts.

He smiled at her gently and put his free hand over hers. They sat that way, feeling each other's heartbeats and staring into each other's eyes.

"My God, you're beautiful," he breathed. "Your hair dances in the wind like fire. Fifty years from now, I'll still remember how you look today."

"This has been a wonderful present," she said, raising her hand to touch his cheekbone. "A wonderful weekend."

He laughed and smoothed her wind-tossed hair. "We'll remember this when we're freezing our buns off in Chicago. You're going to have to keep me warm during those long winter nights. I'm a California boy."

"I'll keep you warm," she promised.

He stroked her hair again. "You'll have a lot to do those two months," he said. "You've got to find us a home, set up housekeeping, get ready for me."

"Tell me again what kind of house you want," she said. She prayed that the job of finding a home would cut at least some of the pain of being parted from him.

He traced his forefinger along the upper edge of her bathing suit. "Lived in and old-fashioned. A big old Victorian, maybe. A place with lots of nooks and crannies that the kids'll love."

"I want it to have high ceilings," she said. "So every Christmas we can have a really enormous tree. Huge."

He nodded. "We'll always make a big deal over Christmas. And always have it at home. Always."

She, too, nodded. Like her, he was an only child. They had both had lonely childhoods, and they wanted a big family.

Evan's parents had divorced when he was five. His mother always left the country at Christmastime, in part to spite his father. Evan had spent most of his early Christmases in Mexican hotels and Caribbean condos.

"I'll find us the perfect house," she vowed.

"I know you will. And before you know it, I'll be home with you."

"Evan," she said, caressing his jaw, "you'll be careful, won't you? If anything ever happened to you—"

"Shh," he soothed, putting his finger on her lips. "Nothing's going to happen to me. I'll finish here and then we'll be together again. Nothing can come between us. Nothing."

"I know," she said softly. "But don't play with any dangerous bugs, all right? You worry me."

He called disease viruses his "pet bugs." They fascinated him, and if she could change one thing about him, that would be it. She wished he'd picked a safer group of viruses to study.

"Nobody's more careful than I am," he said, looking into her eyes. "You know that."

She knew. In the lab he was more deft and expert than anyone she'd ever encountered. She'd never seen him make a mistake. Never. Not once.

"Be even more careful," she said. "Sometimes I start thinking about things like the Marburg virus and Lassa fever, and—"

"Shh," he repeated, touching her lips again. "I'm going to live to be a hundred. No bug's going to keep me from you. Nothing will."

"Promise me that."

"I promise," he said. "Nothing on earth will keep me from you. Nothing. I love you too much. It's a love that can never die. You've got to believe that. Do you?"

"Yes," she whispered, "I believe with all my heart."

4

STOP THIS, she told herself, her hands tightening on the steering wheel.

She forced the memories back. There was no bright, blue African sky here, no crashing waves, no palms with graceful fronds stirring in the wind.

The gray sky had turned darker, the snow fell more swiftly and the ghost white drifts rose on either side of the street. She was in the landlocked heart of America, a thousand miles from any ocean, and she felt trapped in everlasting winter.

She'd left Nigeria a year ago in June, and Evan had died that August. He had been dead almost sixteen months. Why, lately, could she picture him so vividly that it cut like a knife? And why did the coast of western Africa seem far more real than the Chicago suburbs?

It was almost Christmas—was that why she was remembering Evan so vividly? The streetlights of the suburbs were strung with cheery decorations that robbed her of all cheer. Perhaps Evan's plan for a lifetime of traditional Christmases was haunting her, thrusting her away from the painful present.

Veronica was right, Alvin was right, Jerry was right: she must stop living in the past. But how, when the past was becoming more real and vibrant than the present?

Jerry especially was right. Getting through this phase was going to be difficult, and she would need help. She was glad she'd made another appointment with him.

The sky was dark by the time she arrived home. When she opened her door, she heard the phone ringing. Brushing the snow from her coat, she hurried to answer it.

"Carol?" It was Charles, his voice full of anxiety. "You left early today. I stopped by your office. Where were you? Is something wrong?"

Carol closed her eyes, as if she could shut out his intrusive questions. She could imagine the concern on his face. His receding hair gave him a high forehead, and it was always marked by three horizontal worry lines.

Charles's mouth was full and sensitive, and when he was troubled, it twitched. His eyes were watery blue—blue eyes shouldn't remind her of a spaniel's, but his did. Then a wave of guilt swept her for being so critical of him.

"Nothing's wrong," she said. "I had an appointment, that's all."

He sounded relieved. "I wanted to confirm our date on Friday. I'm taking you to Adolphe's. You know how picky he is about reservations."

Her guilt intensified. She had been out with Charles almost every Friday night for the past six months. But when she'd made a Friday date with Mark Martinson, Charles hadn't even crossed her mind.

"I'm sorry," she said reluctantly. "I've made other plans for Friday night."

"But last Friday night you said—"

"Charles, I forgot what I said. I told you I'm sorry. I didn't mean to hurt your feelings."

"For weeks we've had a standing date on Fridays. For months." Hurt vibrated in his voice.

Oh, this is so futile, she thought in exasperation. *I've tried to be kind to him, but I'm only leading him on. I should end it before it goes any further.*

He mistook her silence for anger with him. "I'm sorry," he said abjectly. "I was taking you for granted. I had no right. It was presumptuous. Forgive me, please."

He was impossible. She wanted to snap at him, to tell him not to abase himself, not to apologize. The fault was hers, not his.

"Charles," she said as kindly as she could, "we've been seeing each other for some time. But it's a relationship that doesn't seem to be going anywhere. I think maybe we should let it come to an end."

"An *end?*" he almost wailed. "Carol, you haven't even let it begin."

"There's nothing to begin," she told him. "We were friends—we still are. I hope we always will be. But as for anything beyond that . . ."

"What is it?" he asked. "Someone else? You've found someone else?"

The pathos in his tone set her teeth on edge. "No. There's nobody else."

"You're seeing somebody else on Friday night, aren't you? That's it, isn't it?"

She put her fingertips to her forehead in frustration. "Yes. But I'm not involved with him. And I doubt that I will be."

"If it's not somebody else," he accused, "it's still your husband. Isn't it?"

"No," she said, but then because it was a lie, she added, "yes, Charles. I suppose it is."

Let him know the truth at last, she told herself. *Maybe it'll be a step forward for both of us. We can stop playing this useless game.*

He was silent for a moment. When he spoke, his voice had risen surprisingly. "How can I compete with a dead man? Will you tell me that, Carol?"

She supposed, wearily, that he had every right to be angry. She said, "I haven't been fair to you, I know. I've tried to feel more than friendship for you, but I can't. And you've made it clear that your feelings—"

"No," he said sharply. "I don't think I've made my feelings clear at all. Maybe if I had, you wouldn't treat me like this."

"I just don't want—"

"You've built a wall around yourself," he charged. "I've waited for it to fall down. Maybe it has to be knocked down. Is that it?"

"Charles, no," she insisted. "I just think your time would be better spent with someone else, because I—"

"I've felt this way about you for *years*," he said bitterly. "God knows I've tried to be patient. God knows I've tried not to push you or be demanding or inconsiderate."

"You've been incredibly kind, but—"

"Carol," he said, "don't I deserve better than this? After all this time? Can't we at least talk face-to-face? Don't I deserve that much?"

"There's no more to say," she protested. "And I don't see what good—"

"Oh, there's plenty to say," he countered sarcastically. "There are any number of things that *I* haven't said. I'd like a chance to say them in person. May I come over? Listen to me—here I am begging again, like a pet dog."

"Charles," she said in despair, "don't talk like that. Of course you deserve a hearing. But I'm saying it won't really make any dif—"

"I'll be over," he said grimly. "It's time we were honest, Carol."

He hung up before she could reply. She listened to the relentless buzz that filled the phone line. Then, feeling empty and sick, she hung up the receiver.

She squared her shoulders and forced her emotions under control. So Charles insisted on an audience, did he? Well, she could give him that courtesy at least.

She took off her coat and hung it in the hall closet. Then, restless, she looked around the first floor for Shadow. There was no sign of him.

Outside the sky was black, the snow falling even more heavily. Charles would have a terrible drive getting to her. She hoped it wouldn't aggravate his wounded feelings even more.

Until he arrived, she had nothing to do except wait for him. It was not a pleasant prospect, so she forced herself to go upstairs, to busy herself by searching for the missing cat. She carried a flashlight with her.

She trudged up the long staircase and switched on the light in the upstairs hall. Only stillness greeted her. Every door along the hall was closed, just as when she'd left the house that morning.

One by one she searched the rooms, most of which were empty. There was no sign of the cat anywhere. She called his name, knowing that it was wasted effort.

She looked in the great dusty attic, which was devoid of everything except cobwebs. She made herself search even the least accessible corners. But the cat was not there.

After she'd returned to the hall, she looked at herself ruefully. Her blouse was smudged and her panty hose were torn at the knees. She should change clothes before Charles arrived, and certainly she ought to put on some coffee for him so she wouldn't seem totally inhospitable....

But she found herself standing before the shut door of the tower bedroom, the only place she hadn't searched. Outside the wind had risen, howling, and the old house creaked in reply. She listened to the shrill wind and stared at the bedroom door.

It's foolish to be frightened of a door, she thought. She supposed it hadn't been wise to shut up the bedroom. After talking to Jerry, she realized a great many things she'd done since Evan's death weren't exactly conducive to mental health.

Hanging on to this huge old house was a prime example of unhealthy thinking. She vowed to call the real estate agent first thing in the morning and lower the house's price. She would move into the city, perhaps get a nice apartment overlooking Lake Michigan.

As for the tower bedroom, it was only a room. Jerry said she should go into it, get used to it. "Desensitize yourself" was how he'd put it. And of course he was right.

Nevertheless, when she placed her hand on the brass doorknob, her pulses pounded and her throat was tight with apprehension. She forced herself to turn the knob and ease open the door.

At first, all she saw within was darkness. She slipped inside, reaching for the light switch. Then she noticed the blue light, bright and motionless, dominating the center of the room.

She gasped and dropped the flashlight. She stared across the darkness at the bed. She could see only part of it, silhouetted black against the azure light.

The light was not merely there, she realized in frightened awe. It had *grown.*

The luminescence had spilled out from beneath the bed and now ascended around it in tall, still veils. She could see the black shape of the bed's head, the dark outlines of its posts.

The blue light was static, yet it seemed alive. It rose from the floor in large, motionless tongues of phosphorescent blue. It cast no shadows, shed no glow beyond itself.

Her heart drummed, and her breath caught in her throat. The light surrounded the bed, hiding its legs, its feet, its mattress. It was as if the bed were being eaten by silent azure flame.

She stared as though hypnotized. The blue formed a sort of nimbus around the bed, but did not flicker, flutter, sparkle or flash. Again she was struck by how the glow appeared to be almost a solid thing, a bit hazy but capable of being touched.

Her body stiffened when she saw something small and dark forming at the bottom of the azure glow. The dark area grew larger, took on a familiar shape with pointed ears, then stepped free from the light. Shadow had emerged.

Silently he walked along the edge of the dais that supported the bed. He stood for a moment, staring in Carol's direction. The hall light caught in his eyes, making them glitter pale green.

He moved toward her, then seemed to change his mind. Rather, he stepped back into the light and disappeared once more. Almost immediately, he came back out again, only to creep back inside, vanishing anew. As if he were playing a game, dancing in and out of the still light for her.

Later, she would wonder why she didn't turn and run. She would wonder why she didn't feel terror, scream. But she didn't. Instead she was gripped by an intuition so strong that it overpowered all other instincts.

The cat wove in and out of the light, a dark shape being born out of the blue glow, then merging with it again. *He's showing me it can be done*, she thought in fearful awe. *He wants me to come inside, too*.

Some of the motionless flamelike spires of the azure light were almost four feet tall. If she approached the glow, perhaps she could enter it simply by bending, then stepping inside as the cat kept doing.

Indeed, the cat did seem to thread in and out of the glow for her benefit. His movements were sinuous and mesmerizing, and she watched, powerless to do otherwise.

Suddenly a tingle swarmed up her right arm, prickled her wrist. She looked down and sucked in her breath sharply. The ID bracelet was faintly glowing with the same blue light that appeared to be drinking up the bed.

She touched the fingertips of her left hand to the silver links. The same prickle, almost pleasant, fluttered through her veins. She touched it again and felt the same elvish sensation, as if the silver had somehow come alive.

The cat stepped inside the steady azure brightness and disappeared again. But this time he did not vanish completely, nor did he return. Only his tail was visible, switching slowly, as if taunting her to follow and catch him.

Without thinking, by sheer instinct, she moved to the dais. She bent and touched the cat's quirking tail. It quickly flicked out of sight, vanishing into the light. Then it reappeared again, a few feet farther to her left.

"You tease," she whispered, but she was too intrigued to stop herself. Once more she reached for the cat's black tail, and this time she held it fast. He tried to pull away, as if tugging her nearer to the light.

When she let go of him, all trace of him again disappeared. She studied the light, which streamed upward from the floor of the dais, steadily and seamlessly.

From within the glow, she heard the same sound she'd heard last night, a cat's lonely, plaintive cry. Almost calling to her to follow . . . Part of her mind was paralyzed by the utter impossibility of what was happening. Another part responded almost recklessly.

What have I got to lose? she asked herself, nearly laughing. *If I'm only imagining this, I've gone off my rocker. Why not go all the way? Alice followed her white rabbit into Wonderland. I'll follow my black cat.*

It was utter insanity to entertain the thought that the azure light was real. But if it wasn't real, it couldn't hurt her. She took a deep breath, bent her head and, like one under an enchantment, stepped inside the glow....

ONCE INSIDE THE LIGHT, Carol could hear the cat, but not see him. He sounded near, yet at the same time far away. She no longer felt lighthearted or reckless, and looked about in near panic.

She could see her hands, perfectly normal and agile, she could see her lower body, as well. She was bathed in a shadowy blue light, and she seemed to be standing on absolutely nothing.

Wrong, she thought in both awe and dread. She was standing on azure light, and she appeared to be the only thing in the universe *not* made of light. Its glow, infinite and changeless, stretched in every direction.

She was too terrified to move. She knew that she had stepped straight forward into the light, so the bedroom— and safety—should be directly behind her, only inches away.

But if she began to wander in this never-ending, featureless world, she might never find her way back. Her most overriding desire was to escape, yet something she couldn't explain held her motionless, spellbound.

She had never seen such a wonder, never even imagined it. The softly gleaming blue seemed endless, as if she truly had stepped into a universe composed only of light.

Yet if light was all that existed, it was solid beneath her feet, as flat and sturdy as a floor. She could breathe, and the scent of the air was pristinely fresh, its temperature unremarkable.

There was no horizon in any direction, because there was no distinction between any sort of ground and sky. There was only the unending, slightly hazy light.

The cat cried again, and the noise seemed to come from directly ahead of her. *If I go after him, I'll never find my way back*, she thought in fear.

He cried again, more beseechingly than before. She felt something soft touch her ankles and, startled, looked down. The cat had materialized as though from nowhere, and he was rubbing against her affectionately.

She stared at him in disbelief. He glided against her ankle, purring without cease. Then he moved away from her, walking a few steps forward into the light. He paused and glanced over his shoulder, as if to see whether she was following.

She stood rooted to the spot, not daring to budge from it. Shadow came back, rubbing and purring again. Then once more he stepped away, as though trying to lead her somewhere. He stopped again and gazed back at her, blinking innocently.

Then he turned, staring off into the distance, his ears pricking higher. She looked in the same direction, and her stomach gave a sickening lurch, as if she were in an elevator dropping too swiftly.

There, in the blue distance, stood a figure of a man.

Not any man. Evan. *Evan*, she thought with a thrill of recognition. Her heart seemed to stop, then to bang crazily in her chest.

She could see him only as a dark outline against the light. But it was him; she knew by his height, by the width of his shoulders, the narrowness of the hips. She knew it by his hair, which even at this distance she could see needed trimming.

Shadow turned once more, coming back to her, caressing her ankles seductively with his silky body. His purr thrummed in her ears, but she barely paid attention to him, hardly felt him. Her eyes were on Evan.

For the third time, Shadow stepped away from her, trying to lure her into following, heading in Evan's direction. *Evan,* she thought again, and took a hesitant step toward his distant figure.

But then she heard Evan's voice, strong and vital. "No!" he cried out. "Carol? Stop! Don't go any farther!"

The shock of hearing his voice momentarily paralyzed her. She stared across the distance at him. He, too, stood stock-still.

"Evan?" she asked, tears stinging her eyes. "Evan?" She took another step toward him.

"No!" he almost screamed.

The raw passion of his cry stopped her.

"I don't know what will happen to you," he warned. "Please, Carol, go back!"

But the cat was running toward him now, a black figure bounding soundlessly through the blue.

"Evan?" she called. "Can you come closer? Is it really you?"

"I'll come to you," he said, reluctance in his voice. "But don't move. Do you hear me?"

"I hear," she said breathlessly. She was blinded by tears, and furiously she tried to wipe them away. Through their blur, she saw him heading toward her. His pace was swift, but he held his body tautly.

Shadow met him, then turned and loped softly by his side. The man and cat moved through the blue light, their feet seeming to touch only the glowing air.

A knot burned in her throat, and fresh tears sprang to her eyes. She could see Evan's face now, somber and intent. A sense of marvel filled her.

Then he was before her, only a few steps away. He stared at her, apprehension in his expression. He stood motionless, and she sensed the tension in him.

She started to rush forward, to throw herself into his arms.

"No!" he commanded, holding out his hand as if to ward her off. "I don't know what happens if we touch."

She halted, feeling drunk merely with the sight of him. His wavy brown hair was streaked with gold. His skin was as bronzed as it had been that day at Golwanda Beach, and he looked impossibly beautiful to her.

His eyes were a brighter, more vivid blue than the light that surrounded him. His mouth had a wary set, and his jaw was rigid with self-control.

He was breathing hard, and so was she. *Evan is breathing,* she thought, stunned. She reached her hand to him. He regarded it tensely.

"If I don't touch you," she said, her voice tight, "how will I know you're real?"

"I'm real," he said between clenched teeth. "Maybe if I touch you, you can't go back. I want you to go back, Carol." He stared at her outstretched hand as though convincing himself he really saw it. Shadow rubbed against his legs, twining himself in and out between them.

"The cat touches you," she said desperately. "And you must have touched him. You put the bracelet on his neck. Didn't you?"

He raised his gaze to hers. "Yes. I shouldn't have. But I knew he could go to you, bring you here. You probably thought you were seeing things, right? I shouldn't have put you through that."

"It doesn't matter," she said, her voice trembling. "Oh, Evan, touch me, please. You've touched the cat, and he can go back and forth. Why not me?"

Evan shook his head. He looked so normal, so true-to-life, that it shook her to the heart. He had on jeans, jogging shoes, a tan bush shirt, his favorite belt, the one with the silver buckle. He wore his wedding ring.

Suddenly she didn't care if she ever got back to the tower bedroom. She closed the distance between them before he could protest. She threw her arms around his neck and pressed her lips to his. She was electrified by the realness of his touch.

It was not a phantom kiss—his was not a phantom mouth—and the desire she immediately sensed in him was true and human. He wound his arms around her possessively, and they were arms of flesh and blood, muscular flesh, coursing blood. He kissed her as hungrily as she did him; he was as consumed by joy as she was.

His body was hard against her breasts, the column of his neck strong and warm. She clutched him almost convulsively and lay her face against his chest. Her tears were wetting his shirt. She felt the thud of his heart, heard its muffled beat.

"I can feel your heart," she half sobbed. "Are you really alive?"

"I am in this place," he said, anguish in his voice. "But not over there, where you are. Oh, God, I'm sorry, Carol."

He held her even tighter. "I love you," he whispered against her hair. "I didn't mean to leave you. It was an accident."

"But you've come back," she said, pressing closer to him. "You said you wouldn't let anything come between us, and you didn't. Oh, Evan, I love you."

He drew back slightly, keeping one arm locked around her waist. He touched her face, gently raising it to his. He looked at her for a long moment, pain and regret mingling in his expression.

"I haven't really come back," he told her, shaking his head. "I can only come this far, no farther."

"But what is this?" she begged him. "Where are we?"

"I don't know," he said.

She put her hand over his heart, feeling its strong beat. The tears rose again, and she tried to blink them back. "They said that you were gone, were nothing but ashes."

"I was. Back there. In that world."

"How can you still be alive?"

"I don't know."

"Is this a different world?" she asked. "An alternate universe? What?"

"I don't know," he said again.

He wiped a tear from her cheek. She seized his hand and studied it. It was vital and pulsing in hers, and she stared almost greedily at the familiar white scar at the base of his knuckle.

She gazed up into his eyes again, wishing he wouldn't look so troubled. "Is this . . . the afterlife?" she asked.

A harried expression came into his eyes. "No. It's something else."

She held his hand more tightly. "You mean like purgatory or limbo?"

He shook his head again. "No. And it's not permanent. I can't stay here."

Her marrow turned to ice. "Can't stay? What do you mean?"

"No. Don't cry. This is like a crossroads. I don't know what happens next."

"Evan, I don't understand any of this. Please—"

He lay his fingertip against her lips. "I don't understand, either. But They said that here I might see you again. They didn't say I *would*, but They said it was possible."

He spoke of *Them* with such a mixture of awe and apprehension that she was frightened.

"They?" she asked in alarm. "Who are They?"

He stroked her cheek with his forefinger. "I don't know that, either. Only that They have powers. And I was restless. Too restless. So They opened a gate."

"They? A gate?" she asked, bewildered. "Evan, what's happening? And what do you mean, you were too restless?"

He laced his fingers through her hair. "Your hair, your beautiful hair. I never thought I'd touch it again, touch you, see you. I was someplace where I was supposed to be happy. I wasn't happy."

She gripped his shoulders, which were substantial and warm and hard beneath the cloth of his shirt. "You were in someplace like heaven?"

He shrugged. "It wasn't my idea of heaven. And I can't describe it. They won't let me remember it now. And They won't tell me what happens next. All They let me know was that the cat could go to you, let you know I still exist. And he did. But maybe I was wrong to let him. Carol, you should go back. I got to see you one more time. That has to be enough."

"No," she cried. "I just found you."

"Time is different here," he said earnestly. "I can't stay here, and you can't, either. Go back while you can."

"Why can't I stay with you? When you have to go, I'll go with you."

He took her by the upper arms. "No. You have to go back—now. Right away. They're telling me. It's what They say."

"They?" she asked in disbelief. "They're talking to you? Right now?"

He gave an emphatic nod. "Yes. Not with voices. But I know what They say. I hear them in my mind. They say you should go back now. You have to."

"I won't," she vowed. "I won't be without you again. I couldn't stand it. Wherever They send you, I'll go, too. I don't care if it's bloody hell itself—"

He took her face between his hands. "No. Don't say that. I don't know what it is. It may just be emptiness. Not being. Nonexistence."

"Then stay here," she begged. "And I'll stay with you."

He kissed her, a too brief kiss that almost broke her heart. "That's something you can't choose. Not now."

"Why can't I choose it? It's my life. Oh, Evan, kiss me. Hold me closer. Make love to me."

His muscles tensed. It was as if an electrical shock had jolted him. "Don't say that," he said. "Don't say that yet." He spoke from between gritted teeth, and his voice was pained.

"Evan!" she cried. "What's wrong? What do you mean, *yet?*"

"They want you to go back now," he said tightly. His hands fell away from her. "They make the rules. If you don't go back now, They'll shut the gate forever. You'll be trapped here, and God only knows where I'll be—"

"Evan," she begged, "what's wrong?"

"Go back," he said. "Now. Choose if you'll come again. The cat will lead you. But They say to choose carefully. It's a sort of test. Because if you choose to stay here, there's no turning back. Now, go. Before They take me for good—"

His words were lost in an anguished groan. His body lurched unnaturally erect, then he was hurled to his knees, as if some outside force had snatched him up, then thrown him down in punishment.

She had a terrible intuition that They were hurting him, and it was because of her.

She turned and fled out of the light.

She found herself standing, shaken, in the tower bedroom. The cat sat beside her, calmly licking his paw. Sunlight streamed into the room around the edges of the ragged blinds.

It was no longer night. And the bed stood empty and dusty, illuminated by no other light than that falling from the windows.

5

SHE STOOD stunned. The sun shone so brightly around the shades that she knew it must be close to noon. Yet she had been away only moments.

She looked at her watch. It said 5:45, which was approximately the time she had stepped into the blue light; the hands of her watch hadn't moved. But somehow she had lost as much as eighteen hours. Edging back from the bed, she moved nervously to the door.

The cat stretched, yawned and followed, his pace casual, almost bored. He did not deign so much as to glance at her. He moved so smoothly that his bell didn't make the slightest jingle.

Once outside the room, Carol shut the door tightly. Her mind numb, she looked up and down the barren hall. It was quiet, with sunshine gleaming through the round stained-glass window. Jewellike spots of light fell on the worn carpet.

Everything seemed perfectly normal. Except she had lost all those hours. *And she had seen Evan. Evan was alive.*

Dimly she became aware that her phone rang insistently, but she ignored it. She picked up Shadow and held him tightly against her breast. She closed her eyes and leaned back against the faded wallpaper, mentally and emotionally exhausted.

"Shadow," she whispered, "you took me to him. You really took me to him. Can you take me there again?"

The cat tried to wriggle away. Gone now were his purring and shows of affection. But she held him fast anyhow and wouldn't let him out of her grasp.

The phone stopped ringing. The house almost echoed with silence and emptiness. *I saw Evan,* she thought, still stunned. *I touched him. We kissed. We held each other. It was real.*

Her eyes still closed, she let herself slide slowly down the wall, sink to a sitting position. She clutched the cat more tightly. Her mind careered wildly between joy and terror.

Let go, she heard a strange voice say. But she did not hear the message aloud; it was soundless, heard only in her mind. The voice was low, sexless and without emotion.

Let go.

She opened her eyes and stared into the cat's pale green gaze. He'd stopped struggling, as if such tussling were beneath his dignity. He blinked slowly.

Let go. He seemed to look through her, as though she were as transparent as a square of window glass. A fresh frisson of disbelief swept through her, and she released the cat as if contact with him burned her flesh.

He sprang free, then turned to look at her. He shook one paw fastidiously, as though shaking off the memory of her touch. He gave her the same cool green stare.

"You," she murmured, breathing hard. "What are you? And what's happening to me?"

They have opened a gate. You must choose whether to pass through it. But you must take time choosing. It is Their command. It is how it must be done.

Her mouth curved into a disbelieving smile. At the same time fresh tears stung her eyelids. "Well, this is fine, isn't it?" she asked Shadow. "Now I'm talking to a cat. And better yet, you're talking back."

The cat's whiskers twitched backward a bit, giving him a disdainful air.

There are more things in heaven and earth, Horatio, the voice in her mind said, *than are dreamt of in your philosophy.*

Her tears stung harder, and the corner of her mouth twisted more ironically. "Oh, better and better," she said sarcastically. "A cat who quotes Shakespeare. My sanity's gone, isn't it? I've gone totally mad, haven't I?"

It is always a question of what you believe. The cat half closed his eyes and raised his chin to a supercilious angle. He yawned daintily.

"I want to go back to Evan. I want to go now. What happened to the light?"

He yawned more lavishly. No answer came to her.

"When can I go back to Evan?" she persisted. She was no longer whispering the words, only barely forming them with her lips. "Will you really take me to him?"

You will make choices.

"Choices?" She felt another chill prickle through her. "What are these 'choices'? Why did Evan say it was a test? Is this some sort of trial?"

It goes beyond. It is what They must have and will have.

She narrowed her eyes in cold suspicion. "Who are 'They'? Why did They hurt Evan? Are They evil? They must be."

The cat gave her a haughty look. *There is no thing that's good or bad but thinking makes it so. They will have Their choosing. How else to make you leave? It was you who caused his pain, not They.*

She bit her lip at the thought that she was responsible for Evan's suffering. And she felt a surge of anger toward the cat. He'd brought her to this pass, and she blamed him for creating such chaos.

He seemed to read her mind.

Some go mad if they behold a cat, the voice said. *A harmless, necessary cat.*

"When will you take me to Evan again?" she demanded.

In three days.

"Three days?" she said, swept by dismay. "How can I wait three whole days?"

Ah, said the voice. *That, of course, is the question. To be or not to be, that is the question.*

He turned his back to her and walked away with such arrogance that she was filled with the desire to spring after him and capture him again. She would shake the truth out of him; she would make him—

These aggressive thoughts were interrupted by the sound of the door buzzer. The buzzer was an especially loud, harsh one, and it startled her badly. At its obnoxious noise, the cat bounded down the stairs and disappeared from sight.

Then someone was knocking on her door—no, not knocking so much as banging desperately—and she heard a man's voice calling.

"Carol! Carol? Are you in there? Open up, for God's sake."

It was Charles, she realized in sick alarm. She'd forgotten all about him, and he had been on his way to see her last night. She hadn't been there, and she'd missed her morning class, as well.

She sprang to her feet in growing panic. She didn't want to talk to Charles; she could never tell him what she'd seen, what she had experienced. He would think she had suffered a nervous breakdown.

She clung to the banister, fear and confusion sweeping through her. She didn't dare face Charles at this point. She must marshal her thoughts, her emotions—

But she heard the scratch of a key in her front door. "Oh, heavens," she whispered to herself in horror. "He's gotten somebody to unlock the house. He's come to check on me."

What could she tell him? That she'd been in the Twilight Zone, talking to her dead husband, who was no longer dead? That her bed was being consumed by blue light? That she had established telepathic communication with her cat?

She had no chance to order her thinking or get ahold of her tumultuous emotions. She stared down the stairs as the front door swung open. Charles, accompanied by her real estate agent, Hal Gleason, stepped inside.

Charles was the first to look up and see her at the top of the stairs. His pale eyes widened in surprise. She realized that she must appear a fright, that she'd never changed clothes after grubbing about in the attic, searching for the cat.

"Carol," Charles said in alarm. "Where were you? What happened?"

She smiled feebly and tried to think of a plausible answer. *I was in Shadowland,* she thought.

"Professor Glendower," Hal Gleason said, staring up at her. "Are you all right? We called, but there was no answer. Professor Harvey here was worried...."

Charles was looking her up and down, clearly discomfited. She was aware that her skirt and sweater were dirty with dust and that the knees of her panty hose were torn. Her face was probably smudged, as well, and for all she knew, she had cobwebs in her hair.

"I came over last night," Charles said, his forehead creasing with worry. "Your lights were on downstairs and in the upstairs hall. I checked your garage. Your car was there. But you didn't answer the door. I went to the drugstore to phone. You didn't answer."

Hal Gleason loosened his muffler. He was a wizened little man with a pointed nose. He stared at her over the tops of his glasses, which were fogged. "Professor Harvey was concerned when you weren't at the university this morning," he said carefully. "And I'd been trying to get through myself. I couldn't reach you."

"It's not like you not to call in if you're going to be absent," Charles said. "That's why I phoned Gleason here— I was concerned about you."

She nodded and tried to appear grateful. Charles's soft face was filled with anxiety, and he held his hat in his gloved hands. The foyer light gleamed on his balding head.

Her knees felt shaky, and she wished with all her heart that these two men would go away. But they stood gazing up at her in puzzlement and expectation.

"Your clothes are dusty," Charles said, almost accusingly. "Your stockings are torn. Are you all *right*, Carol?"

She was struck by sudden inspiration. "I was locked in the attic," she said, and forced herself to give a derogatory laugh. "Did you ever hear of anything so foolish? I was looking for the cat. The door slammed shut, and there I was, trapped."

"You were locked in the attic?" Charles said. "All night? Good grief, Carol, I was worried to death about you."

"It was nothing," she said, and wiped a patch of dust from her sweater. "But I just got out. Minutes ago. I finally found a screwdriver."

"Well," said Hal Gleason, unbuttoning his overcoat, "I'm grateful we showed up. What if you couldn't have gotten out on your own? You might have been trapped there for who knows how long?"

"You must be cold, tired, hungry," Charles said. "Couldn't you hear me when I knocked last night? I came back two more times to check on you."

"Oh, yes," Carol said, blithely lying. "But I couldn't do anything. The windows are nailed shut, and I didn't want to break anything. I called and knocked, but you didn't hear."

"You're still a bit shaky," Charles said, his worry lines deepening. "I can see it."

He started up the stairs, as if she were some invalid that he would kindly guide down.

She damned her own nervousness. She shrugged and made a foolish, helpless gesture with her hands. "I feel more stupid than anything. Sort of like Mrs. Rochester, locked in the attic."

Hal Gleason blinked. "Mrs. Rochester?"

"She's a character in a book," Carol explained. "Her husband kept her in the attic because she was as mad as a hatter."

The comparison, she thought, was perhaps all too apt; she was convinced that her husband was still alive, which must make her madder than any number of hatters.

"Poor darling," Charles said.

He'd pursed his lips and spoken to her as if she were a child. He put one arm around her shoulders. Snow was melting on his overcoat, and he smelled of damp wool and mothballs.

"Come downstairs," Charles said, trying to help her down. He treated her as gingerly as if she were a hundred years old. "We'll get something hot in you, clean you up and call the university so they'll stop worrying."

"I appreciate your concern," she said with a tight smile, "but what I really need is just a bath and to crawl into my own bed."

This was a lie, of course—she was not tired at all—but she hoped her words would make Charles stop his unwanted ministrations. He led her to the living room, then paused, drew out a perfectly folded handkerchief and wiped her cheek tenderly.

"I was afraid you didn't want to see me," he said softly. "I was afraid at first that you were ignoring me."

"Nonsense," she said with a little toss of her head. But it was true she hadn't wanted to see him and still didn't. "What I really need to do, of course, is go into the bathroom, freshen up," she reiterated. "You can be on your way. It was nothing, only a silly accident."

"I'll make you some coffee," Charles said. "Or would you prefer tea? Hot chocolate, perhaps. Maybe a nice piece of buttered toast? Or toast with jam? Oatmeal? Would you like a piping-hot bowl of oatmeal? Oatmeal's very good for you."

I'd like to be left in peace, she wanted to retort. *I have so much to think about—too much to think about. Stop hovering over me and mothering and smothering me.*

But he seemed intent on staying, and she was too shaken to argue, especially in front of a third person. "Just instant coffee," she managed to say. "The kettle's on the range, and the coffee's on the counter."

She excused herself and went into the downstairs bathroom. She stared at herself in the mirror over the sink. She did indeed have a cobweb in her hair, and her face was unnaturally pale, and she did feel distinctly unsteady. No wonder Charles was going into such fits of overprotectiveness.

But what she noticed most about her image was the faint, smeared remnant of her lipstick. Her lips were slightly swollen from the pressure of Evan's mouth upon her own, and her lipstick had been kissed away. Her mouth still tingled from Evan's touch.

She touched her fingertips to her lower lip. She could *see* the evidence of Evan's kisses; she could still *feel* it. She pushed up the arm of her sweater and noticed that she still wore Evan's bracelet, the one that was supposed to have been destroyed.

She looked into her gray eyes, which seemed haunted, but thoughtful and alert. Hers was not the face of a just-awakened dreamer, nor was it that of a woman just emerged from a major hallucination.

She was certain that she had seen Evan. And if it had been possible for her to be in Evan's arms again, why was it not possible for a cat to tell her that in another three days she might go to him again?

But sane people did not communicate with cats, and in the real world, the dead did not return, warm, vital and full of passion.

She sighed in anxiety and dashed cold water on her face, ran a brush through her hair, dusted the worst of the dirt from her clothing. Once again she eyed herself in the mirror. She was white faced, which made her freckles stand out, but otherwise she appeared remarkably normal.

Charles had made himself at home in the kitchen. He'd thrown his overcoat over the back of a chair, and his hat and gloves lay on the counter. The gas fire danced beneath the kettle, and he had mugs and spoons on the table and was actually making toast.

But Hal Gleason wasn't going to stay. "I'll leave you two alone," he said, slipping on his gloves again. "But I'll be over later tonight, Professor Glendower. I have good news for you. You've had an offer on the house."

Carol went nearly rigid with shock. She stared at the little man in disbelief. "What?" she said.

Gleason nodded soberly. "You'll be pleased. A couple from Michigan. They didn't quibble about the asking price. They're offering you the full amount. I'll be over this evening with the contract. I'll call first."

"What?" she repeated. Her blood drummed in her ears, which seemed odd, for she was cold all over, as if all her pulses had ceased working.

Gleason nodded, watching her reaction closely. "Yes," he said. "They want the house. They'll pay full price. They'd like possession as soon as possible. They want to get to work on renovations."

"They want possession of my house?" Carol asked in a choked voice.

"Yes, my dear. I'll talk to you about it later."

"That's splendid news, just splendid," Charles said enthusiastically. "It's about time you unloaded this white elephant, Carol. It'll give you a new lease on life."

She stared at Hal Gleason, shocked. She knew he saw her alarm, even if Charles didn't. Gleason was an observant man, a student of human nature, and she suspected that he knew she'd been lying about the attic.

She struggled to act naturally. "Well, of course I'll consider it carefully," she said.

"Thanks for your help, Gleason," Charles said in a take-charge tone. "I appreciate it. I was concerned about her. And I can't tell you how glad I am she's finally getting this house off her hands."

Charles began buttering a piece of toast. "Sit down, sit down," he told Carol. "Gleason can let himself out. He knows the way."

"I certainly do by now," Gleason said, and gave Carol a stern look.

He can tell I don't want to sell the house, Carol thought with guilt. She nodded to him; he nodded back curtly. She watched him leave the kitchen, and she let Charles seat her at the table so he would stop hanging over her like a worried nursemaid.

She picked up her coffee cup and was chagrined to see that her hand shook. Charles saw, too. He sat down across from her, took her free hand in his.

"Poor baby," he said. "Would you rather go to bed? I could bring all this up to you on a tray. Would that be better?"

"Charles, please don't," she said, struggling to hang on to the ragged threads of her patience. "I should go to bed. But I don't need all this fretting over me. I just need to be left alone. If you think we have to talk, make it another time. Please. I've had a hard night."

A night that shook my heart, my sanity, all I've ever believed was true. But I was with Evan. Go away and let me savor that. Let me try to understand what's happening.

Charles squeezed her hand harder. "I really was afraid you were just avoiding me," he said. "And when you didn't show up this morning, I actually got frightened. I was afraid perhaps you'd—you'd . . ."

His words faltered. His thick lips twitched, and he shook his head. His hand tightened around hers even more inescapably.

"You were afraid I'd what?" she asked warily. She pushed the coffee away, the plate of overly buttered toast, as well. She wanted no food or drink, only solitude.

Charles trained his pale blue eyes on hers. "I was afraid you might have done something to yourself. Turned on the gas. Taken an overdose of pills or something."

"Charles!" she said, truly shocked. "You know I'm not that kind of person. I'm not self-destructive."

He leaned nearer. "The way you've acted toward me lately, darling," he said earnestly. "Growing more distant. Saying you're going to see someone else. Then, last night, saying you and I should break off—this is self-destructive behavior."

She tried to wrest her hand away, but he held it as if in a death grip. The absurdity of what he said filled her with resentment, but she was frightened, as well. How appalled he would be if she told him about Shadowland. And how certain he would be that she had lost her mind.

She straightened her spine, lifted her chin. "What I said to you was simply the truth. I'll always think of you as a friend, but nothing more. I still love my husband."

Charles dragged her hand to his chest and held it over his heart with both hands.

"But he's dead, Carol. He's been dead for sixteen months, so you can't love him the way you'd love a living man. I love you the way you need to be loved, body and soul."

He practically growled the words, and he tried to make his expression fierce with passion, but he looked like a baby seeking to make a ferocious face. She was embarrassed for him, but he had exhausted her, and she'd had all she could bear.

"He's *not* dead," she shot back without thinking. "He *is not* dead. I've been with him. Last night, I was with—"

She stopped in midsentence. The horror in Charles's eyes cut off her words.

"What?" he asked. All fierceness drained from his expression, and for a moment he looked merely stupefied. "What did you say?"

Oh, God, was it only her imagination, or was a strange gleefulness beginning to shine from his eyes?

"Nothing," she lied. "I said nothing."

"What were you doing in the attic last night?" he demanded. His tone was gentle, but firm, like a concerned parent's. "Going through his things? Trying to run from me and hide in your memories of him?"

"No," she protested. "And let go of me. You should go home now, Charles. I'm touched by your solicitude, but I need to be alone."

She stood, trying to wrench her hand free, but he rose with her, and his grasp was surprisingly strong. He stared down at her, and his eyes was full of satisfaction.

"Did you hear yourself?" he challenged. "You actually said he wasn't dead. You said you'd been with him. My God, Carol, you need help, and I'm the man to see you get it. I'll see you through this."

"I don't need help," she said, desperate to escape his bullying, his clinging. "I don't want you to see me through anything."

But instead of letting go, he pulled her closer. "Is that how you got locked in the attic?" he persisted. "It was a bit Freudian. You were afraid to see me, because you knew this moment was coming?"

"No," she insisted, trying to twist away from him. "Stop touching me."

Dimly she realized that she had never known he was this strong. He was tall, of course, but he'd always looked so fleshy and unathletic that it had never occurred to her that he could overpower her.

"Carol," he told her, "you *want* to be touched. You love me. You just can't admit it. You're afraid, because you know no one will ever love you as much as I do."

"Stop," she told him, "don't say that."

She tried to push away from him, but he only caught her and held her more fast than before. His arms imprisoned her so tightly that it pained her to breathe.

"This is what women want, isn't it?" he said with a bitter smile. "I was too much the beggar, too much the supplicant. Perhaps you never thought me capable of passion. I am. Great passion."

He lowered his face to hers, even though she was trying to writhe from his grasp. His lips descended on hers, and his mouth was thick and cold and wet. He crushed her against the fuzzy wool of his sweatered chest, and the force of his kiss bent her head back.

She was shocked, frightened, and his touch filled her with such disgust she thought she might choke on it. His tongue worked against her clenched mouth like a warm, fat worm trying to wriggle its way in.

But more than anything, she was hot with resentment that he'd dared try to erase the memory of Evan's touch with his own, unwanted caresses. She summoned all her strength and thrust herself away from him.

"Get out of my house," she ordered. She was shaking again, her knees feeling almost insubstantial beneath her, her balance precarious.

"I think we should both get out of this mausoleum," he said with feeling. "God knows it's not done you any good. Come to my place. I'll call Gleason to bring the papers over there."

"Your place?" she asked, confusion fuddling her brain. "No. Absolutely not. Papers? What papers?"

He took a step toward her, and she edged away, working her way toward the hall. He had decided to assume a masterful mode with her, and he seemed to like it.

Charles smiled at her as he would at a wayward, yet lovable, child. He kept moving toward her. "The papers on the sale of your house. You'll be much better once you're out of here."

She couldn't leave the house. It was her only gateway back to Evan. The house and the cat. The cat, she thought irrelevantly. Where was he? Back in Shadowland with Evan? Or here somewhere, watching this whole terrible scene with his cool green eyes?

"I'll never sell this house." She flung the words at Charles. "I'll never leave it—never."

"Don't be silly," he told her, his eyes locked with hers. "You're not a silly woman. You're intelligent and reasonable, and if you look at this situation with intellect and reason, you can see I'm right. Pack your things. We should get you out of here as soon as possible."

"No!" she cried. "I'm staying. You leave. I don't want you in our house anymore."

She'd backed into the hallway, and inexorably he'd followed, and he was moving closer again. He paused for a moment, and the self-satisfaction gleamed in his eyes once more.

"Don't you see, darling?" he asked. "How can you call it 'our house'? You've never shared it with anyone. Except that cat. And you should get rid of that troublesome cat. I'll get you a real pet. A little poodle, perhaps."

Get rid of the cat? Panic filled her at the prospect. She put her hand on the newel post of the railing. He took another step toward her, as if he meant literally to back her into a corner.

"Stop—stop stalking me," she ordered. "I want the cat. I want my house. I'll stay in this house. Leave us alone."

"You can't stay in the house," Charles said, his voice condescendingly sweet. "Gleason says the new owners want immediate possession. Let them have it, and get on with life. Pack your things. Your place is with me. And mine's with you. Stop fighting it, Carol."

He put his hand on top of hers. He looked into her eyes again, smiling down at her. "I'll make you well, Carol," he said. "I'll make you whole again."

She snatched her hand from beneath his. "I'm not the one who's sick," she said passionately. "I told you, I won't move in with you. I'll never feel that way about you. Or any other man—except Evan."

"Evan's dead," Charles said, his smile dropping and the hard light coming back into his eyes. "Evan's a handful of ashes in some bloody, godforsaken sea. But I'm alive, and I love you, and you love me, if you'd only let yourself—"

She could stand no more. She fled up the stairs, praying that he wouldn't follow.

"You can't run away from facts," Charles cried after her. "The facts are that he's dead, he's going to stay dead and you'll never see him again. To think anything else is madness."

Then she thought she heard his footstep on the bottom stair and turned in fright. She saw the determination in his eyes. He meant to have her. She turned away again, trying to run faster.

But she could feel him closing in behind her, and his words echoed in her mind: *"The facts are that he's dead, he's going to stay dead and you'll never see him again. To think anything else is madness."*

She felt his hand close around her ankle, and her knees buckled with fear.

"Evan!" she screamed, and even as she fell, she stretched her hand desperately toward the tower bedroom.

Then there was the pain of hitting the stairs the wrong way, of falling down them in a helpless sprawl, Charles's hand still fastened leechlike on her ankle. And then there was no pain at all, only blackness closing over her mind.

6

SHE HAD a long, complex, lifelike dream of spending a week's holiday with Evan on the Serengeti. It re-created, exactly, the trip they had taken just before she had to return to the States. The trip had been an extravagance, but Evan had thought they should visit the Serengeti before she must leave.

Their second afternoon they had seen a lioness bring down a wildebeest. The chase was brief and swift, the end violent. Carol had looked away when the wildebeest's graceful legs buckled, not wanting to witness the bloody kill.

She shut her eyes tightly and pressed her face against Evan's chest. He put his arm around her shoulders protectively, holding her tight. He, of course, watched the whole drama without flinching.

"It's over," he said after a moment. "It's okay now."

But when she raised her eyes and saw the wildebeest lying still, reduced from a beautiful animal to bloody meat, she looked away again. She had their camera, but she wanted no pictures.

She had snapped dozens of photos of the reserve's wildlife—zebras, storks, crocodiles, monkeys, hippos, even elephants and a lone, ill-tempered baboon sitting on a riverbank, picking fleas. But for some reason she felt a deep resistance to recording the wildebeest's savage death.

That night she told Evan, "You're the better scientist. It's strange. I've seen films of big cats bringing down prey so often I can't count the times. I never thought it'd bother me in real life. But it did."

Evan had just stepped from the bathroom, where he'd showered. They were staying in one of the guest chalets at the permanent camp; the lodgings were excellent, the nearby restaurant superb—they had even had champagne with their supper.

He was naked except for a white towel knotted around his narrow waist. His tanned skin, still slightly moist from the shower, gleamed with vitality. His chest was broad and beautifully muscled, shadowed with curly brown gold hair.

She sat on one of the twin beds, clad in one of the short, filmy nightgowns he loved for her to wear. He smiled down at her, his special one-sided smile of affection that he never gave anyone except her.

"Why worry about it?" he asked. "It was gory. Not like the death of some lab animal. And it wasn't on film. It was really happening."

She shook her head and went back to brushing her short hair, which was still damp from her own shower. "I don't know. I just thought I'd be more objective. I *used* to be, I'm sure."

He sat down behind her and kissed her on the bare shoulder near the strap of her gown. "Death is natural," he said. "It's just an ending. This one just happened to be particularly nasty. Don't think about it."

She turned to him, feeling inexplicably troubled. "But I do think about it," she said, looking into his jewel blue eyes. "I'm a scientist. For years I've trained myself not to be emotional about natural processes, not to take them personally. What's happened to me?"

He took the brush and laid it aside. He put his hands on her shoulders. "We've been talking about having kids," he said quietly. "That's what's happened. You've reprogrammed yourself."

She drank in his handsome face. It was gilded by the dim glow of the lamp, and his wet and tousled hair gleamed in the light. She tried to smooth a cool lock of it away from his forehead, but it immediately fell back.

"Reprogramming," she said with mocking resentment. "You make me sound like a computer."

"You don't feel like a computer," he said, running his hands down her arms, then up again. "And you don't look like one." He gave a growl of sexual hunger, deep in his throat. "But if you are one, you make my hard drive ready."

She laughed. "You're incorrigible."

"I'm serious," he said. "We're thinking of creating a new life. A woman who's about to create life looks at death differently. I think you take it as a personal affront. You're one force. It's the opposite."

Oh, she thought in admiration and yearning, that was Evan, able to see clearly and straight into the heart of the matter.

She put her arms around his neck and inhaled the fresh, coconut scent of his soap and shampoo. "Evan," she said as seductively as she could, "let's get started now. Tonight. You're right. I do want to think only about life. I want your child inside me. Now."

He rubbed his forehead against hers. "Not mine," he said. "Ours. And not yet. We've talked about it."

She went silent, knowing he was right, even though she was still filled with yearning. They had both decided it was wiser to wait. If she conceived a child now, she and Evan would be separated for part of her pregnancy, when she returned to the States.

He didn't want to be away from her while she was pregnant, nor did she wish it. Besides that, they had the thorny problem of a two-career marriage. They both agreed it was best that her career in Chicago be firmly entrenched before the first child came.

But that meant such waiting, such planning, such caution and cold logic. Sometimes she felt as if she couldn't wait. She loved microbiology, but she loved Evan far, far more.

"I can't stand putting off getting pregnant for three more years," she murmured, then nuzzled his bare collarbone. "You be the family genius. If we can't start now, let's start as soon as you get back to the States."

He drew back from her slightly, gazed into her eyes. "You're the most delicious little flirt in the world," he said. "But you know we can't. We wait until our second year in the States. Then I get you pregnant that October so you won't have to teach the last month and you have the summer to enjoy the baby. And you keep working full-time until the next little bundle of joy comes along, which will be exactly two years later."

She gave him her sexiest pout. "I've changed my mind. I don't want everything on a timetable. Why do I have to establish a career? I'll be working only part-time for years and years and years with all those children...."

He smiled but shook his head. "Because you're good, and because if anything ever happens to me—"

If anything happened to him? If he died? The mere thought frightened her so much that a chill darted up her spine and her body stiffened.

"Don't even say such a thing," she said. "You have to promise such a thing would never happen."

He tried to draw her back into his arms again, but she resisted. She looked deep into his eyes. "Promise," she said.

"I can't promise such a thing," he said. "It's a natural process, as I said."

She felt like a fool, but tears sprang to her eyes. "No. What would happen to me without you? I couldn't bear it. You can't ever leave me that way. Promise."

"Carol," he said in surprise. "This isn't like you. What's wrong, honey?"

She didn't know. It was as if she'd had a terrible glimpse into a future without him, and such a possibility shook her so deeply that she felt as vulnerable as a child. He was right; this *wasn't* like her.

She was never flighty, emotional, melodramatic. Her cool-mindedness and rational approach had been the despair of all her suitors before Evan. "You think like a man," one had told her, half in admiration, half in disgust.

But here, in this lovely chalet surrounded by the wonders of the Serengeti, she was swept with such a cold sense of foreboding that she could barely fight back her tears. Soon she would be on a distant continent, and Evan would still be in Africa.

Long weeks, a great ocean, huge stretches of land would separate them. She could stand that because it would eventually be over. But to be parted by something as absolute and endless as death? She felt suffocated by dread.

Her lower lip trembled. "I will not," she said, "*allow* you to leave me, Evan Glendower."

"Carol," he said again in concern. "What's got into you, sweetheart?"

"I don't know," she said, shaking her head and trying to regain control of her runaway imagination. "But your work *is* dangerous, and—and I don't know ... Maybe that's why I couldn't watch the wildebeest d-d-d—"

She couldn't bring herself to say the word *die*. Instead she dissolved into hopeless weeping and was furious at herself. How childish Evan would think her, how silly and weak.

But he didn't rebuke her, didn't laugh. He drew her against his bare chest and kissed her beneath the ear. "I'll never leave you," he vowed. He kissed her throat. "Do you want me to promise? I promise. Death itself isn't strong enough. How's that poem go? 'I love you so much that Death itself will die.' Don't cry, baby. Don't cry, sugar."

She had believed him. And he had kissed her and whispered endearments and caressed her until fear had fled and desire had taken its place. Softly he'd slipped the straps of her gown from her shoulders so that it fell in a silken heap about her waist.

With his sure hands and questing mouth he'd made love to her breasts, her thighs, the tender center of her femininity. When he'd entered her, her need for him burst every boundary, and both her body and mind seemed to shatter into light, like a shooting star turning into flaring sparks.

She held him fast, her arms around his neck, her legs clasping his hard, bronzed body, her mouth pressed hungrily to his. Outwardly and inwardly she rocked with his powerful thrusting, dissolving into him, becoming one with him.

Afterward, she lay glowing and exhausted in his arms, and he made sleepy jokes about how they would die that way, on their eightieth anniversary, spontaneously combusting as they made crazed love.

"They'll find these two charred, frail little sets of bones on the scorched sheet," he murmured, and kissed her naked shoulder. "Locked together in the missionary position—if we're feeling conservative. The children will be shocked, even as sophisticated as they are. The grandchildren will be chagrined. The great-grandchildren will be embarrassed. And the great-great-grandchildren will blush..."

She could feel his warm, muscled, naked length against her; feel his breath fanning her shoulder; hear the lowness of his voice, husky with satiated desire.

He kissed her shoulder again, his lips lingering against her cool skin. Outside, from beyond the compound fencing, came the strange cries of the African night. But she and Evan were safe and together in their pristine little chalet, the lamplight still shining on their uncovered bodies.

She tried to turn to him, to touch him intimately again, to taste his lips and whisper words of love.

But the memory, so real only a moment before, grew cooler, dimmer, more distant. She tried to grasp it again, but it fled away like water flowing and disappearing into darkness.

She awoke to find herself in a strange room, with Veronica sitting at her bedside. The room was dim, the venetian blinds tightly shut, but winter sunlight streamed through them. She knew immediately it was a hospital room, but couldn't understand why she was there.

Veronica rose, hovering over her, her face full of concern. She put her warm hand over Carol's pale, cold one, which rested on the starchy bedsheet.

"Evan?" Carol asked, bewildered. Her eyes searched the ceiling's corner shadows, as if she might find him there. "Where is he? He was just here."

"Shh, honey," Veronica whispered. "It's just me here. You had a fall. You passed out. Can you remember?"

Carol frowned, touched her forehead gingerly, then winced. She could feel the tenderness of a bruise just above her temple, at the hairline. She had only a fuzzy, dizzy memory of a fall, so vague it didn't seem important.

Something far more crucial nagged at her mind.

Evan. Evan was alive in Shadowland!

Shadowland. The memory came rushing back: Evan, tall and well and whole, moved toward her. He came through an unwavering mystic blue light, a black cat loping at his side.

He was there, he was alive, he was real. She remembered being crushed possessively in his arms, kissing his mouth, clinging to him so she might never allow him to be torn away from her again.

"Evan?" she repeated, panic rising. She had been exiled from the blue light and from him. Some mysterious force called *They* had driven her away, shut her out. But the cat said she could go to him again in three days.

She had been with Evan. He was still alive but she could only get to him through the light. The light was in the tower bedroom. The cat would lead her, but not for three days.

Three days? How long had she been unconscious? She tried to sit up, but a bolt of pain shot through her temple. With a muffled moan, she sank back against the pillow. She clutched Veronica's hand spasmodically. "How long have I been here?"

"Honey," Veronica said, worry in her voice, "it's five in the afternoon. Stop worrying about it."

"What day?" Carol demanded, turning to her, hoping Veronica couldn't see the terror in her eyes. She was frightened to death that she'd been there for more than three days. What if she'd missed finding the way back to Evan? How could she ever survive his loss a second time?

"It's Tuesday," Veronica reassured her, "the same day that you fell. Now, stop worrying. Talk to me. Can you tell me your name?"

"Of course. Carol Ann Blair Glendower."

"Can you recite the alphabet? Will you do it?"

Dutifully she complied. She answered Veronica's other questions: her address, what classes she taught and when they met, the past five American presidents, the names of the Chicago baseball, football and basketball teams.

"Great," Veronica said. "Let me buzz for a nurse. They said as soon as you really came to—"

Fearful suspicion jolted through Carol. "*Really* came to? What do you mean?"

Veronica pushed the white button that would summon the nurse. "You've been having what they call 'variable consciousness.' You'd be out a while. Then you'd be able to talk, but as though you were only half-awake. Then you'd drowse off again."

Carol immediately grew wary. "I talked?"

Just as she knew, without doubt, that she had found Evan alive in Shadowland, she also knew that she must tell no one. They would think she was utterly mad.

"Yes, you talked," Veronica said. "You said some far-out things, too. You pretty near scared Charles and me to death."

"Charles?" Carol asked, recoiling. "What's he got to do with this?"

"Honey, he was with you when you fell. Don't you remember?"

Carol strained to recall, her heart beating hard. In a muddied flow, the memory came seeping back. He had nagged and wheedled her, tried to browbeat her, almost forced himself on her.

"Charles . . ." she said, her voice tight. "I was trying to get away from him. He followed me up the stairs. He grabbed my ankle. *He* made me fall."

Veronica laughed softly. "Charles? You've got to be kidding. He said you weren't acting yourself and flounced off from him. You fainted or just plain fell on the staircase. He tried to catch you—"

"He grabbed me," Carol said stubbornly, for she knew the truth of it. "I wouldn't have fallen if he hadn't come after me—"

"Charles?" Veronica repeated in disbelief. "Honey, you must have hit your head harder than we thought."

Carol started to protest, but then a stout, middle-aged nurse appeared, crackling with authority. She peered at Carol's pupils, tested her reflexes, grilled her with questions and made her recite the alphabet again, as well as the presidents.

After the nurse left, a doctor whom Carol didn't recognize came. He was rotund, balding and had a rather ridiculous walrus mustache of graying brown. His plastic nametag announced that he was Dr. Felix Sternberger.

He had the brusque and authoritative air of a man who thinks he knows all the answers. He asked the same stupid questions about her name and the alphabet and the presidents. He made her play something resembling patty-cakes with him.

She had to let him shine a light into her eyes and tap her knee with a rubber hammer. He asked if she could stand. She could, although she felt humiliated in the skimpy hospital gown. He made her walk a straight line and balance on first one foot, then the other.

Meticulously he made notes and peppered her with still more questions. Did she experience any nausea, weakness or tingling? Did she have any drowsiness, change of vision, headache?

Carol answered everything, trying to disguise her growing impatience. The man's overbearing way made her edgy, and she realized that in a sense he was The Enemy. He in particular would doubt her experience in Shadowland, and if he had any inkling of it, he would probably commit her somewhere for a nice, long rest.

So she behaved, and even forced herself to smile. No, she wasn't nauseated; her vision was fine, she wasn't sleepy, weak or tingly. Her head hurt slightly, but no more than was natural after striking it as she had.

She sat on the edge of the bed, and he regarded her as he might a bug in an insect exhibit. "Hmm," he mused, staring at her until she almost wriggled in discomfort. "Hmm."

He drew a set of X rays from a manila envelope and held them to the light. Carol realized that the black-and-white skull in the picture must be hers. The words "Alas, poor Yorick, I knew him well" popped into her mind.

The quotation made her think of the cat, with his cryptic Shakespearean phrases. Her cheeks grew hot with embarrassment and guilt. If Sternberger and Veronica knew she'd exchanged thoughts with a black cat, they would cart her off to a rest home in a minute.

Sternberger turned to her again, narrowing his small hazel eyes. "You *seem* to be fine," he said, irritation in his tone. "The X rays show no indication of damage. You have no physical symptoms except the headache, which is, of course, to be expected."

So why are you staring at me as if I'm a freak? Carol wondered nervously. *Did I say something when I was half-conscious? About Evan? About the tower? The light?*

"However," Sternberger said, confirming her worst fear, "your variable consciousness, your earlier drowsiness, your irrational statements—"

"What irrational statements?" she asked, perhaps too quickly.

He gave her a grave, superior look. "Reportedly, you insisted that your late husband was still alive. There was some incomprehensible mention of a cat, a bed 'full of blue light.'"

Carol's cheeks burned more hotly. She glanced nervously at Veronica, who didn't meet her eyes. She turned back to Sternberger, forcing herself to seem as calm as possible.

"It must have been a dream," she said between her teeth. "Yes, I remember a very vivid dream. Yes, it was about my husband."

"Your late husband," Sternberger amended coolly. "You do understand he's dead, don't you?"

She took a deep, shaky breath. "Of course."

One of Sternberger's graying eyebrows rose dubiously. "Can you tell me how long he's been dead?"

She nodded, feeling as if she were walking a knife-thin edge. "Yes. Sixteen months."

"Of what did he die, if I may ask?"

"Ajuba fever," she said, hating the words. "He was a microbiologist. He was finishing up an assignment in Nigeria. They were trying to isolate the virus. It was a highly lethal one."

"I see," Sternberger said with a sagacious nod. "And what became of his body?"

A lump formed in her throat, hard and sharp. She tried to ignore it. "He was cremated. It was the law. Because of the virus."

"I see," Sternberger said. "And I see, as well, you still wear his ring? On the left hand, as you did when he was alive."

"Yes," she said. "I do."

Sternberger's gaze fell to her wrist. "And his identification bracelet, too."

Her heart took a frightened leap. She'd forgotten about the bracelet. It was still around her right wrist, oversize and too masculine for her. She put her hand over it, as if to protect it from Sternberger's prying eyes.

"I found the bracelet again, just lately," she said, her heart beating more wildly. "I wear it. Yes."

Sternberger smiled superciliously at her. "You claimed a cat brought it to you. Do you recall that?"

She raised her chin and smiled back, just as cavalier. "Yes. I remember dreaming it. As I said, a very vivid dream."

His demeanor hardened. "Have you ever before confused dream with reality?"

"Never," she said. "My field is science. I'm hardheaded, if you'll excuse the expression. I'm not a fanciful person."

"Hmm," he said in his maddening way. "Well, I should like to keep you here for twenty-four hours. The fact that your state of consciousness did vary, that you did utter irrational thoughts—both these indicate your injury may be more serious than it appears superficially."

"For twenty-four hours?" Carol asked in dismay. "Why? You said the X rays looked fine. I want to go home—now."

"And I want to keep you here," Sternberger said. "A person with even a mild head injury should restrict activity for that period. And not be left alone."

"I can rest at home," she said rebelliously. "In fact, I can rest far better there. I don't want to stay here. I refuse to stay here."

"I thought you prided yourself on being a logical woman," Sternberger said with sly smugness. "If your powers of reason are indeed unimpaired, you'll see the wisdom of my suggestion."

"As a logical woman," she retorted, "I don't know why I should pay to lie down in a hospital when I can do it free at home. Why should I pay five dollars for an aspirin when I've got a bottleful in my medicine cabinet? My powers of reason are just fine, thank you, so I'll let them lead me out of here."

Sternberger's nostrils flared. "You are stubborn," he said pompously.

"Yes," she said, looking about the room. "I am. Where are my clothes? Veronica, will you drive me home? I'm checking myself out of this place."

Veronica, who had been silent during the whole exchange, looked first at Sternberger, then at Carol. Then she walked to a small closet and opened the door. She took Carol's sweater and skirt from their hangers.

"If you insist on going home," Sternberger said, "I insist that you have someone with you for the next twenty-four hours. Otherwise I will not be held responsible. I will not be blamed if something goes wrong. I will not be dragged into a malpractice suit."

"Malpractice suit," Carol said scornfully. She watched as Veronica got her lingerie from the metal dresser's drawer.

"What did you do to your panty hose, girl?" Veronica asked, staring at the torn knees.

"It doesn't matter," Carol answered. "Throw them away. I'll do without."

"The only way I'll release you," Sternberger warned, "is into someone's care, do you understand?"

"Fine," Carol answered. "I'll find someone."

She had no intention of finding anyone, of course. She wanted to be alone in her house with her new knowledge of Evan. To see the tower room again. And to find the cat. That cool, illusive, supernaturally wise cat.

"Very well," Sternberger said with a disapproving sigh. "I was told you'd probably be this way. I will release you to Professor Harvey's care."

Displeased surprise shot through her. "You mean Charles? I will not be put in Charles's care. I won't have it."

Veronica gave her an eloquent look that told her she was protesting too much. "I'd volunteer myself," Veronica said, her voice studiedly casual. "But it's my mother's birthday tonight. We're giving her a surprise party. I'd wiggle out of it, but I'm the hostess. I've got no wiggle room."

Carol drew in a long breath through clenched teeth. *Don't seem stubborn, don't seem hostile,* she told herself. *Above all, act as rationally as possible.*

She regarded Dr. Sternberger modestly, her eyes full of innocence. "I don't particularly want a man in my house overnight," she said. "People would get the wrong idea. Professor Harvey might get the wrong idea."

"He's assured me that he'll be the complete gentleman," Dr. Sternberger said. "He knows you aren't yourself. He's sworn not to take advantage."

She was silent a moment, her lips pressed together.

"Oh, come on, honey," Veronica said apologetically. "It's only Charles. If he turns into Don Juan, I'll send Alvin's brother over to cool him down. Just give me a call."

Carol no longer trusted Charles, and she didn't want him in her house. He would either nag and bully, or he would apologize and hover over her until she wanted to scream. She didn't want him thrust into her life, free to roam her house, trying to ferret out her secrets.

She wanted the house, the tower and above all the cat, wherever he was, to herself. Charles would pry, Charles would question; Charles would invade and destroy any chance she had to gather her thoughts.

"Just who are you," she asked Sternberger coolly, "to assure me what a gentleman Charles will be?"

"I am his physician," Sternberger informed her. "And his cousin-in-law. I therefore know I can trust him, and, as I say, I will release you into his care."

A put-up job, Carol thought angrily, and she tossed Veronica a resentful glance. Veronica rolled her eyes, as if to say, "Don't look at me. I didn't do it."

"He called you in?" Carol demanded.

"He didn't want you in the hands of some emergency ward hack. He brought me in on the case because he was concerned about you."

She bit back a sharp answer. "Very well," she said with a polite resignation she didn't feel. "I suppose Charles will be watching over me. But then I'll be on my own. And consult my own doctor."

"He didn't know who your doctor was," Sternberger said silkily. "So he called me. You may feel free to consult me again. Sometimes the seriousness of a head injury doesn't make itself known for days, even weeks. Be on the alert for drowsiness, confusion, behavior changes or any bizarre thoughts."

Bizarre thoughts, she thought with apprehension. *If you only knew, Doctor.* But she only nodded and said nothing.

Sternberger bade her a rather stuffy goodbye and left the room. Carol stared after him. "Lord," she said in disgust.

"He's just the sort of person Charles would have for a doctor. Hand me my bra and slip, will you?"

Veronica did, but her face was troubled. "Are you sure you should go home? Maybe it would be easier to stay here."

"No," Carol said, "I want to be in my own house. Alone. I'll send Charles packing as soon as I can. I will not have that man playing nursemaid to me."

"Carol," Veronica said with a worried frown, "aren't you being a little, well, hard on Charles? I mean, he does care for you a great deal. And he did bring you here after you fainted or fell or whatever happened."

"I told you," Carol said, stepping into her half slip, "I wouldn't have fallen if he hadn't grabbed at me. He was obnoxious. He was talking like a person possessed."

"Charles?" Veronica said doubtfully.

Carol stared at her friend. She could tell what Veronica was thinking: *Carol's got this all wrong. Charles would never act like that. Carol's memory is warped and her thoughts are, in Sternberger's word, bizarre.*

"You don't believe me," she said, hurt.

"He was scared to death for you," Veronica stated. "He brought you to the emergency ward in his car. He called his own doctor. He called me. And the way you were talking—well, it scared me, too."

Carol slipped into her skirt and fastened it. "Why?" she asked, wanting the facts. "What did I say?"

Veronica made an impatient gesture. "All this babble about finding Evan in a world of light, and that he wasn't dead. And when Charles tried to tell you he was, you got angry and even more incoherent."

Veronica paused. "He was almost in tears, the poor man. I told him to leave until you were more yourself again. He's been making phone calls. Arranging to have your classes covered. Postponing your real estate appointment."

"My real estate appointment?" Carol said, jarred by the remembrance.

Veronica nodded. "Yes. Real estate." She put her hand on her hip. "Carol, Charles told me that you've got an offer on your house. A good one. But that you told him you didn't want to sell."

"I—I—" she stammered "—I'm rethinking it, that's all."

Veronica sighed. "You don't want to rethink it. You want to get rid of the place and start a new life. Carol, you're my friend, and I'll be frank. You've been doing and saying some strange things for the past little while. After seeing Charles this afternoon, I'm starting to come around to his side. He may be the best thing that's ever happened to you."

Carol looked her in the eye. "You think I'm coming unglued, don't you?" she challenged. "You and Charles both."

Veronica didn't answer immediately. She stared at the floor for a long moment. "I think you could use some help," she said at last. "Didn't you use to run around with a shrink? Jim Bratling or something like that? Maybe you should talk with him. Yeah, I'm worried. I don't want you to go off the deep end."

Carol looked at her friend in disbelief. *I'm already off the deep end, according to you,* she thought. *You don't understand. None of you. I've got to get back to Evan. I've got to get to Shadowland.*

But at that moment, Charles appeared, his shoulders slumped, a hangdog expression on his face. Wordlessly he came to her, put his arm around her.

She tried not to stiffen in revulsion at his touch. "It's going to be all right, darling," he told her. "I'm sorry I got you upset. I'll look out for you. Everything will be back to normal soon."

She closed her eyes tightly and thought, *I am not insane. I am not insane. I am not insane.*

7

"CHARLES, YOU CAN go now," Carol said firmly. Veronica had driven her home, with Charles faithfully following in his BMW. But Veronica stayed only long enough to see that Carol got into her flannel pajamas and into bed.

Charles was sitting at her bedside, like a devoted nurse out of some Victorian novel. Hurt crossed his face, but the set of his mouth was stubborn.

"I won't leave you," he said. "Felix said you shouldn't be alone."

She squared her jaw. "It wasn't fair to set your own doctor on me. Especially if he's your cousin, too. I suppose he knows we've been seeing each other?"

Charles shrugged and ran his hand over his thinning curls. "He's an excellent physician. And he's right. Head injuries are tricky. In high school, one of the players on our football team got a concussion. He seemed perfectly fine all week. But in the next game—"

"I don't care about some high school football player," Carol warned, trying to hang on to her patience. "All I want is my privacy."

"In the next game he got hit in the head, and he died," Charles said righteously. "Your brain can be swelling, slowly, insidiously. X rays can't tell you that."

She fought back a shudder. What he said was true, of course. She'd known a boy in college who had been in an automobile accident and struck his head. For ten days he had appeared fine, although perhaps a little too high-spirited. On the eleventh, he collapsed, and when he came to, his left side was paralyzed.

"I'll check with my own doctor tomorrow," she promised. "In the meantime, I'm supposed to rest, and frankly, I can't rest while you're hanging over me."

Once again he looked wounded. "You've kept too much to yourself lately," he accused. "Right now, you need someone. Whether you admit it or not."

Careful, careful, her logic cautioned, *he's playing games, and so are you. Don't be the one to slip.*

She sighed tiredly. The tiredness, at least, was genuine. "Charles, you've been wonderfully kind," she said. "I don't mean to sound ungrateful. But you're partly right. I'm not used to having people around. It's stressful for me. You think you're helping, but you're really not."

"And you think you need to be alone, but you're wrong," he countered. "No, Carol. Resign yourself. I'm here to take care of you, and I intend to do just that."

She felt as if she were in a chess game and every time she moved Charles could put her in check. He was determined to stay, and if she made a scene, he would say her agitation was a danger sign, all the more reason for him to keep watch.

She suppressed another sigh. She reached for one of the books on her bedside table. If she could not put him out of her house, at least she could shut him out of her notice.

"You shouldn't read," he said in his best lecture tone. "It'll make your headache worse."

She didn't answer. She stared at the words in the book, but they swam in her vision. Her temple pounded, sending darts of pain through her head.

"You're squinting," he said. "Are your eyes bothering you? That's a warning symptom, you know. Why don't you lie back and close your eyes? Give me that book—I'll read to you."

Before she could object, he commandeered the book. He frowned. "What's this? *The Sudan?* You're reading about Africa? Really, Carol, that's not wholesome. You dwell in the past too much. Let me find something more suitable."

He began poking through the haphazardly stacked books. "*Out of Africa,*" he said, and made a *tsk-tsk* noise. "*Tales of the Serengeti. Death Is a Door, Life Does Not End, Thresholds of Existence.*"

He gave her a stern look. "Books on the paranormal? These all look like books on the afterlife."

"They are," she said defensively. "I'm just reading them for fun."

"Fun?" he said in distaste. "Really, darling, it's a good thing I'm here. No wonder you're acting odd if you're filling your head with this nonsense."

"I'm not acting odd," she shot back, but she knew the paranormal books were another strike against her. She had checked them out from the public library after Shadow had brought her Evan's bracelet.

"I'll just take these away," Charles said, sweeping up the volumes. "And get something more soothing. Where do you keep your books?"

She wanted to scream. She wanted to rise out of bed, brandish the table lamp like a weapon and drive him from her house. She wanted him out of her house and out of her life forever.

"Down in the dining room," she said tightly. "It's a sort of makeshift library."

He rose. "Just lie down," he said. "I'll be back in a few minutes."

He strode out of the room as if he, not she, owned the house. Her head pounded viciously. The thought of

Charles poking about her beloved home, pawing through her books with his soft hands, filled her with repugnance.

She should steal downstairs, slam the heavy dining room door behind him and lock it, trapping him inside.

The thought was so deliciously perverse that it alarmed her. What was happening? She was thinking of snaring Charles and imprisoning him, as if they were characters in some horror?

She was sure Charles had snatched at her on the stairway, making her fall. That is, she was *almost* sure. Why did the fantastic—Evan and Shadowland—seem so real and alive in her memory, while the argument with Charles was fuzzy, broken, dreamlike?

Her headache banged more mercilessly, and the faded wallpaper of her room suddenly seemed to have a pattern of double roses instead of single ones. The doorway shimmered and developed a twin. The dresser with its single framed photograph of Evan became two dressers, two photos.

She shut her eyes, which were suddenly hot with tears. Hadn't Felix Sternberger warned her that vision problems meant something was wrong with her brain? What if she had only imagined Shadowland, had only imagined that Evan was alive?

The tears burned more fiercely. Was she merely escaping into a pathetic delusion? Had she mistaken wish for reality because she was too weak to face reality itself?

Suddenly she felt a weight on the bed, near her feet. Her eyes flew open, and she saw the black cat. Rather, she saw two black cats, one solid, the other like a ghost cat, joined to it and glimmering.

"Shadow," she whispered, and reached to touch him. She shouldn't have moved. Fresh pain shot through her skull. And the cat moved just out of reach, then sat and regarded her with his pale green eyes.

She fell back against the pillow and tried to focus on the cat, whose double image danced in her mind. "Shadow," she pleaded. "Are you even real? I can't tell what's real and what's not anymore."

"We are such stuff as dreams are made of," said the low, sexless voice in her mind, *"and our little life is rounded with a sleep."*

She turned her face to the pillow and tried not to weep. She felt the weight leave the bed and heard the faintest jingle of a bell.

She knew that if she looked again, the cat would have vanished. Perhaps he had never been there at all; she no longer knew.

CHARLES RETURNED with a book of essays on science. He reproved her—gently, of course—for living all alone in such an empty, echoing house.

Her books weren't even completely unpacked, he chided, and some of her furniture was covered by sheets. The place was fit only for ghosts, not a living woman.

She didn't tell him that she'd thrown the sheets over the furniture because sixteen months ago she'd commissioned painters and wallpaperers to come in to refurbish the place. She'd canceled them when Evan had died. She'd never bothered to remove the sheets. They'd somehow seemed fitting.

In a droning voice, Charles read an article about the eardrum tissue of the frog. She did not like opening her eyes because everything she saw now seemed aggressively double, making her dizzy and slightly sick to her stomach.

She grew drowsy, as well, although she didn't want to sleep. She was haunted by the thought of lying asleep while Charles wandered through her house, searching and spying. But at last she could resist no longer and sank into a heavy, languid slumber.

She dreamed, as she always did lately, of Evan.

ONCE AGAIN her dream was so faithful to past events, it seemed like the reality happening to her all over again. On her last night in Ibadan, they had made love slowly, yet desperately, wanting the night to go on forever, trying to ward off morning, when they must part.

"I think I love you too much," she'd told Evan, half in tears, as they lay together in the tangled sheets.

He framed her jaw gently with his hand. "No," he said, his eyes hazy with desire. "It's not possible to love too much."

But she was frantic with need for him, sick at the thought of leaving, already missing him. "Yes," she whispered, feeling frightened and superstitious. "My grandfather was a minister. He used to say it was a sin to love the things of this world too much. That we'd be punished for it."

He smiled the one-cornered smile that was for her alone. "Your grandfather may have seen only part of the picture."

She snuggled against him, savoring his closeness while she could. "I mean it," she said earnestly, tracing his cheekbone with her forefinger. "I love you too much. I love you more than anything on earth—or in heaven. That must be wrong. What if it is?"

"What if it isn't?" he said, and stroked her lower lip with his thumb.

"What do you mean?"

"Transcendence," he said in a low voice, and gave her his lazy, sexy smile again.

"What?"

"Transcendence," he repeated. "If love is strong enough, true enough, maybe it rises over the limits. It triumphs over the negative, over all restriction."

She didn't quite understand what he meant, only that it was lovely. "Explain," she said wistfully.

"It's like what you had engraved on my ID bracelet," he said. "Real love is eternal. It goes beyond time and space. It goes beyond anything we know or can even guess."

She was still apprehensive. She nestled closer to him yet. "My grandfather would say we're setting up false idols."

"I don't love you as a false idol," he said. "I love you as a real woman, that's all. Isn't that what I should do?"

She moved her head on the pillow so that her brow rested against his. "Well," she said reluctantly, "we do get awfully carnal for true love, don't we? My grandfather used to say that sex was for procreation, not recreation."

He laughed and brushed a kiss across her lips. "My, you're the little puritan tonight. Did you agree with your grandfather? Do you regret that we, well, kind of romp around a lot?"

She slid her arm around his neck possessively. "I didn't agree with him. I didn't understand why it couldn't be for both. When we're having sex, I feel like I love you, I love the world, I love the whole universe."

"Exactly," he said and kissed the tip of her nose.

"But still," she said and kissed his jaw lightly, "it scares me sometimes. Maybe we'll have to pay a terrible price for this someday."

He laughed again and drew her more tightly into his embrace. "You really are a puritan tonight, love. When I get to the States will you be dressed in black and holding a muzzle loader? Will you have me thrown in the stocks for lust unbecoming a pilgrim?"

She laughed softly, but felt sad at the same time. "I'm just on edge," she told him. "Because I have to leave in the morning. Two months apart. How will I stand it?"

He kissed her lips. "Love is stronger than time."

"You'll be thousands of miles away," she persisted. "How will I go on?"

"Love is vaster than space," he said, and kissed her again.

His tongue darted against hers, and his hands crept silkily down her body. She arched against him hungrily.

They had made love once already, and their bodies were still musky and slightly damp with the exertion. But she knew they were going to make love again, with even greater deliberation and more exquisite fervor.

"Enough philosophy," he growled, trailing kisses down her throat. "Action's the thing for tonight."

She would never be able to explain what the two of them had experienced that night. She would never even try. It was as if they'd gone far beyond ordinary experience to another higher, more intense plane.

"I love you" was all she could say as their bodies locked like two halves of a perfect whole. "I love you. I love you. I love you."

"Could you eat some nice green pea soup?"

It was Charles's voice, treacly with concern.

"You should eat something. Can you eat something?"

She turned away from the sound, pretending she hadn't heard it.

"Carol, don't play possum. I saw your eyelids flutter. Wake up, dear. You know Felix said it was a bad sign if you were too drowsy."

Oh, God, a bad sign. A bad sign of what?

She wanted to sink back to her dream. She wanted to be in Evan's arms again, back in the rumpled sheets in their bedroom in Ibadan.

But Evan was dead and gone forever.

No. Evan was alive and waiting for her in some alternate universe that could somehow open its gate in the tower bedroom.

An alternate universe? That was insane. It was insane and her head hurt insanely; she felt as if a spike of broken glass had been driven through her temple.

"Carol? Can you hear me? Are you all right? Are you in pain? Do you want me to call Felix, dear?"

She forced herself to open her eyes, then wished she hadn't. Two Charles Harveys hovered over her, their fishy mouths pinched in twin worry. She couldn't completely fight down the groan that rose in her throat.

He bent nearer. "Carol? Your eyes aren't focused. Can you tell how many fingers I'm holding up? Can you count my fingers?"

A blurry forest of pink fingers seemed to waggle before her eyes. Four? Eight? Six? She could not tell.

His voice rose in alarm. "Carol? How's your headache? Is it better? Worse? Tell me, dear."

"I want Evan back," she said. She meant her dream.

"Sweetheart, I know, but you've got to come to terms with that. I'm here. I'll help you get through this. We'll get through this together."

"Charles," she said between her teeth, "would you please just get me an aspirin?"

He bustled away. She couldn't see him clearly, but she had a vision of him wearing a ruffled apron, the better for fussing over her. She couldn't remember ever feeling this ill.

Something really was the matter with her brain, she thought in confusion. Her head throbbed, her eyes saw double if not triple and she could not shake off a sense of sick drowsiness. She couldn't allow this to happen to her, because she must think clearly. She must think with absolute perfect clarity, because . . . because . . . why?

Then Charles was back, stuffing aspirin into her mouth with his fumbling fingers, forcing her to drink and spilling water on her face, her pajamas, the bedclothes. She sputtered and tried to wave him away.

But his awkward hands were on her again, scrabbling at the buttons of her pajama top. "No," she protested, "no." But his hands were inescapable. She felt the top being pulled open, the air striking her dampened breasts.

"No!" she cried, but her voice sounded small and far away.

"I have to get you into something dry, dear," he said.

He was trying to wrestle the pajama top completely off her. As sick as she was, she heard the change in his voice.

"Oh, Carol," he said thickly. "How beautiful you are."

"No!" she cried, and from somewhere deep within, she found the strength to strike at him, strike hard. She felt the back of her hand connect with his face so forcibly that her knuckles stung. She heard him gasp, but he let go.

She pulled the halves of the pajama top back together as tightly as she could and rolled away from him. "If you touch me like that again, I'll kill you when I'm well," she said, her voice shaking. "I mean it. Don't you ever touch me like that. Only Evan can do that, dammit."

"I'm sorry," he said in a petulant tone. "You misunderstood. I was only trying—"

"Leave me alone," she ordered with such ferocity it surprised her. And then, because she was inherently a woman of logic, she said, "If you touch me again, I'll file a suit against you, Charles. A sexual harassment suit. You'll never work at a decent university again."

"You misunderstood," he repeated with a whine.

She knew she had scored a vital point. But the effort had exhausted her. Drowsiness tugged at her, tried to suck her down like a dark tide.

SHE HAD HOPED that sleep would take her back to Evan. But this time it did not. Instead she was seated in a huge, featureless room that appeared ancient and empty. She sat on the stones of the floor. She was cold.

Facing her was the black cat. He sat erectly and neatly, like an Egyptian statue. He regarded her with his steady emerald gaze.

"This isn't fair," she said. "I can't tell what's real and what's not anymore."

The familiar voice, haughtily mocking, spoke in her mind. *To sleep, perchance to dream; perchance to dream; ay, there's the rub.*

"Where's Evan?" she demanded, shivering. She seemed to be wearing pajamas, and the top was wet. She hugged herself to stop shuddering. "Where is he?"

The cat blinked slowly. *That undiscovered country.*

"What undiscovered country? How can I get to him? How can he get to me?"

The cat sat motionless. *No traveler returns.*

"If I go to him, what happens?"

No traveler returns.

"He said that They'll send him someplace else. Beyond Shadowland. Where is it?"

No traveler returns.

"Who are They? What are They?"

There is a destiny that shapes our ends.

"Who are you? What are you? Are you one of Them?"

The shadow is strongest where light is great.

She clenched her teeth in frustration. "And you move between different worlds? Different planes of existence?"

'Tis true I have gone here and there.

"You can never give a straight answer," she said bitterly. "Only crooked ones."

The voice grew haughtier still. *How poor are they that have not patience!*

"How can I be patient? We're dealing with life and death—of the man I love."

I have told you. They will have Their Choosing.

"Their choosing," she said in exasperation. "What choosing? And why?"

We cannot all be masters. Truth is truth.

"Can't you say one thing to help me instead of bewilder me?"

The cat regarded her for a long moment, coolly looked her up and down. Then he ducked his head and slowly raised it again, as in a condescending nod. When the voice spoke, it spoke slowly, with great deliberation, as if what it said must be remembered.

Our doubts are traitors, and make us lose the good we oft might win.

He paused and settled his pale, unwavering gaze on her eyes. *Virtue is bold, and goodness never fearful.*

Then he rose, turned his back to her and walked away, his black tail switching languidly. He moved as quietly as a shadow, and into the shadows he disappeared.

She sat alone and in despair, cross-legged on the cold stones. She looked around the great, empty chamber and could not tell if she was in a dungeon or throne room, a crypt or a cathedral.

The stones of the floor were chilly and drab, as were those of the high walls. The vaulted ceiling was lost in shadows, and she could see no door, no window. Silence lay heavy on the air.

"Shadow?" she said. Her voice sounded small and timorous. "Shadow?"

No answer came. The silence seemed to swell more oppressively, weigh on her more heavily. The beat of her heart was fast and thready. She didn't want the evasive cat who sometimes quoted—and misquoted—Shakespeare or spoke in riddles of his own devising. She wanted Evan, the one being on earth she had trusted without reservation.

"Evan?" she cried, pierced through with need for him. "Evan? What should I do? How can I get to you?"

The words hit the barrier of the stony walls, echoing hollowly. "Evan . . . Evan . . . what? . . . how? . . . Evan?"

The massive silence closed in on her again. It seemed to last for aeons. The dusky walls began to waver before her eyes, to swim and shimmer, their rock starting to dissolve into nothingness.

Then, from between the stones of the floor, a tiny, oily voice arose. No, a chorus of voices, twining in a way that was somehow both shrill and soft at the same time, like fingernails teasing the edge of a blackboard.

Like the cat's voice, these spoke more to her mind than her ears.

"Beware, beware, beware!" the small, twisting voices cried, so sharply that they hurt her head.

"Beware of what?" she asked helplessly, putting her fingertips to her temples.

"The cat, the cat," the voices warned in their muted squeal. "Evan says to beware the cat. Evan says. Evan says."

"Evan?" she asked, full of foreboding. "The cat? Why?"

The voices rose a notch, twining more intensely. "The cat may be no cat. The cat may be no cat."

She felt as if crooked pins were being pushed into her skull. She shut her eyes against the pain. "Of course he's no cat," she said shakily. "But what is he?"

The chorus broke apart, became a dozen different whispery shrieks.

"A demon!"

"A demon!"

"Not a cat. A hound from hell!"

"A demon!"

"A devil!"

"A fiend!"

"A demon in thy view!"

"Evan says—"

"Evan knows—"

"Evan wants—"

"The fiend wants—"

"The foul fiend wants you—"

The tiny voices jabbed at her skull, bit at her brain. She covered her ears in the vain hope of shutting them out, but they babbled on, their screeches tangled together.

"Beware—"

"The cat is a tempter—"

"He comes from hell to tempt you—"

"Corruption—"

"Death and corruption—"

"Don't go to Evan."

"Evan says, 'Turn back.'"

"Evan says, 'Beware the foul fiend.'"

"Evan says, 'Choose the living.'"

"Evan says, 'Charles loves you—'"

"Evan says, 'Choose Charles—'"

"Charles will love you—"

"Charles will care for you—"

"Charles will complete you—"

"The cat comes stinking of death—"

"Charles is life—"

"The cat comes trailing death—"

"Charles is your destiny—"

"The cat stalks—"

"The cat slinks—"

"The cat slays—"

"—Slaying you—"

"—Tempting you—"

"—Damning you—"

She pressed her hands harder against her ears, but the voices skirled on, flying at her like cutting shards of glass.

"Stop!" she screamed back at them. "Stop it! Who are you? Where are you? Where's Evan?"

For a moment that seemed at first blessed, then ominous, there was quiet. Then the voices gave a hissy little sigh in ragged chorus. When they spoke again in chorus, even higher than before.

"We are Evan's brothers. His brothers. His sons. His legacy. He sent us to you . . ."

Even the hard thrumming of blood in her ears could not drown them out. She had bitten the side of her mouth so hard that it bled, and she could taste her own blood, thick and coppery, in her throat.

The pain in her ears, mouth, throat, mind was so harsh it made her harsh in turn. "Who are you?" she demanded, almost spitting the words. "*Where* are you?"

"We are Evan," the twisty little voices shrilled. "We are his last wedding gift to you. We are what is left of Evan. We are here, beneath the stones."

The chorus broke apart again, and the separate little voices assaulted her, squealing and seething.

"The stones whereon the cat walked—"

"The stones where the cat did bring you—"

"The stones, which are the cat's sole god—"

"And all the mouths beneath the stones—"

She could bear no more. Thrusting her fingers down into the powdery mortar that held the darkest, nearest floor stone in place, she wrenched it upward, not caring that it tore her fingernails, bloodied her hands.

The stone heaved loose with a weary sucking noise, and paralyzed, she held it, leaden, in her hands.

She stared in horror at the black, raw ground she had unearthed. From the dark, damp soil, ringed round by stones still in place, writhed countless pale worms, slimy and stretching upward as if straining toward her.

They sang to her in their hushed, high, discordant voices:

"Beware the cat—"

"Let Evan rest—"

"Charles is life—"

"The cat is death—"

They wriggled, glistening in the dim light, and they sang to her.

She dropped the rock and screamed.

"Stay away from me!" she implored raggedly, crying and trying to fight down hysteria. "Keep away! And keep the cat away!"

Then the stones were gone, the shrill, cacophonous singing was gone, the dream was gone and arms held her tightly.

Evan, she thought in relief. *Oh, Evan, thank God. Hold me. Make the horror stop.*

"The cat—" she said brokenly, trying to explain. "Oh, help me. They said the cat— And the cat is all I have ..."

"It's all right, darling," a deep voice said. "It's all right. I've got you now."

She sagged with relief against his chest. But the chest against which she rested her cheek was too fleshy, even beneath its thick sweater, and the arm that held her did not feel truly safe.

With a sick shock she realized she was not clinging to Evan, but to Charles.

He lowered his face and placed a moist, lingering kiss on her ear. "It's all right," he repeated breathily. "I've got you now."

8

CAROL WRENCHED HERSELF from Charles's arms and threw herself facedown on the pillow, clutching it and trying to keep from weeping. Her head pounded, and she felt a grinding in her skull, as if the worms' shrill voices were drilling through to her brain.

"Carol?" Charles said, his voice vibrating with devotion. "Darling?"

She felt his hand massaging her shoulder and jerked away. There was no escaping him. His hands were on her, hauling her into a sitting position, pulling her against his chest, pressing her to him in a suffocating embrace.

"Leave me alone," she said, trying to push him away. She wanted to wrest free, to hit him with her fists if necessary, to scream for him not to touch her.

But her body had no strength; her head ached too horribly, and when she opened her eyes, her vision swayed and danced, making her sick to her stomach.

"What about the cat?" he asked, his breath hot and moist in her ear. "What about the cat, love?"

He wore a fuzzy sweater, and its fibers itched her and blocked her breath. She had to cling to him to keep the room from spinning around her drunkenly.

Think clearly, her tortured mind ordered. *Act rationally. You're in trouble, great trouble.*

"Charles," she managed to say, "call my doctor. I'm worse. If you care for me, help me."

He pulled her more tightly against him, and his sweater's hairs seemed trying to climb into her nostrils, her mouth. He had a warm, oversweet smell, like fruit that has grown too ripe.

"Sweetheart? What about the cat? You were tossing and muttering about the cat as if you were scared to death—"

The room spun more swiftly, and she had to grip his shoulders more firmly. "My head hurts. I see two of everything. I feel sick."

"Tell me about the cat, precious," he crooned, his hands running over her back. "You said he was a demon?"

"No!" she cried. "*They* said he was. They were trying to make me doubt him. When he said I mustn't doubt—"

"Sweetheart, you're making no sense. Hush, now. It's all right. I have you."

She marshaled all her reason, all her willpower. "Call my doctor. His name is Turner. Dr. Robert Turner. And Dr. Bratling. Jerry Bratling. Call Veronica. Tell her I need her."

"That's right, darling. Hang on to me just as tight as you can. I'm here for you. The cat can't hurt you."

"Charles," she half sobbed, half snarled, "get me help."

"I have," he cooed. "I've called Felix. He'll be here. Charles is taking care of you, dear. Charles takes care of his sweet girl."

"I'm not your sweet girl," she said, her fists tightening on his sweater. "I'm Evan's girl."

"Shh, sweet love. You're my girl now. Darling sweet. Sweet darling."

Her head ached hellishly. The room rocked and spun, even with her eyes shut. She wanted to thrust him away from her, but she had to hang on to him, to keep herself from falling off the edge of the world.

He kissed her ear. "I'll take care of you," he said.

I'm this man's prisoner, she thought, sick with dread.

SLEEP STALKED HER, and there was no fleeing it, no escape. Sleep, at least, rescued her from Charles. It took her, blessedly, to Evan. Once again it was as if she were reliving events in perfect detail.

She and Evan had met on a Monday. That evening he had taken her to supper at the restaurant of an American hotel. The food was good, the wine excellent. She knew that they were going to make love afterward. They both knew it.

He was a distractingly handsome man, tall and well built. His blue eyes were so beautiful that they would have made a less masculine face boyish and pretty. But he had a strong nose, an angular jaw, and his mouth seemed permanently set at an irregular angle.

She was vaguely aware of the murmur of other people's conversation, the clink of silverware and crystal and the strains of recorded music. The song was "If Ever I Should Leave You."

"I read your article on the mutation of the yellow fever virus," she told him.

His gaze traveled slowly from her eyes to her lips and back again. "I had to do something until I met you," he said. "So I mucked around in the guts of mosquitoes. Will you marry me?"

The question should have been absurd, but it wasn't. She knew somehow that she *was* going to marry him, even if it seemed to fly in the face of reason.

But she smiled demurely and said, "You're mad."

He gave her his one-cornered smile, the one that would be hers alone.

"I didn't know you'd be a redhead. I'm pleasantly surprised. Bewitched, in fact."

"Quite mad," she said. "Totally."

He raised his wineglass and stared at the rich cabernet. "Much madness is divinest sense," he said. "That's from a poem, I think. Some philosopher said that once we were each a half of a whole. But then somehow we got separated and born alone. So we spend our lives searching for our other half."

"And?" she asked, a bit breathlessly.

He looked at her over the edge of his wineglass. "I thought he was a damned fool. Until you walked into the lab today. Congratulations. You just gave true meaning to Philosophy 101."

She tried to appear cool and ironic. "Do you always come on this strong?"

He cocked one eyebrow sardonically. "Nope. Not at all."

"So why are you doing it now?"

"Because I didn't know I was searching for you until I found you. You're the Not Impossible She."

She laughed again. "You're crazy. What are you talking about?"

He reached across the table, picked up her hand and studied the freckles sprinkled across her knuckles. "A redhead," he mused. "With freckles yet. This will be interesting. Thank you, God. The 'Not Impossible She' is from another poem. She's what every man dreams of. Prays for. Do you like kids? Of course you do."

"In fact, I do. If I ever get married, I want hordes. I was an only child."

"So was I. What constitutes a horde?"

Her hand in his felt both natural and enchanted, an intoxicating combination. "A horde is four. Two boys. Two girls."

"Precisely," he said. "I want a big, old rambling house. So do you, I'll bet. No modern slab on a manicured yard for you. Right?"

She took a deep breath, her heart pounding hard and fast. She had an inherent attraction to large, eccentric Victorian houses, and she was repelled by the sterile lines of modern architecture.

"Right," she said.

"I read your résumé before you came," he said, studying her hand again. "I thought, well, this sounds like an intriguing woman. More than interesting. Too good to be true. Do you know that our interests are practically identical?"

"You're making that up," she said, but she made no move to draw her hand away.

"No," he said, running his thumb meditatively over her knuckles. "Camping. Traveling. Wildlife observation. You went to the Galapagos two years ago. To see the tortoises. I went three years ago."

She smiled at the coincidence. "Really?"

"Really," he said. "You went wilderness camping on a tidal island off the coast of Georgia last year. I went two years ago. Same island. Sapelo."

"You didn't," she protested, delighted. "You're just saying that."

"You did your master's thesis on the Marburg virus," he said. "That's what I wrote about in my senior honors seminar. You minored in English. So did I. You spent your junior year in England. So did I. I did Oxford. You did Birkbeck. I bet I know where you went on your first break."

"You couldn't know," she protested, but she had the eerie feeling that he did.

"Stratford-on-Avon," he guessed. "Because you thought you should, right?"

She stared at him in pleased wonder. "How could you know that?"

He raised her hand and brushed a kiss across the back of her wrist. "Because I did, too. I thought I should. And you were disappointed, right?"

"Right," she said. "I was expecting a quaint, unspoiled village—"

"And you found a tourist trap selling Shakespearean salt and pepper shakers and cheap ashtrays."

"Exactly!"

"But you've been to Stratford in Canada," he said. "I saw that on your résumé, too. You did the Shakespeare festival up there last July. I did it in June. We just missed each other."

"That's uncanny," she said, "I can't believe it."

"And I'll bet your favorite bar in Stratford is Bentley's. Right?"

"Of course," he said, as she nodded. "And the most astonishing thing about the town is—?"

"The flower gardens. *Everywhere.* And was your favorite play—"

"*Midsummer Night's Dream*? Right? And the actor you can't forget was—?"

"That totally wild man who played Bottom. And did you buy the—"

"CD of the music? Yeah, I love it. You, too?"

"Oh, *yes.* And there's that wonderful little—"

"Bakery? You ate breakfast there?"

"Every day. I wanted a day of nothing but breakfasts. And I bought my all-time favorite T-shirt there. It says—"

"If it says Now I Must Believe in Unicorns, then you have to marry me."

"My God, it *does* say that—"

He kissed her hand again. "Okay. We get married. And you know what? I think that finding you is more marvelous than finding any unicorn."

"You have to stop talking like this. This is only our first date."

His gaze captured hers, and the blueness of his eyes jolted through her, made her feel as if the earth were quaking.

"This isn't our first date," he said. "You know that."

She looked more deeply into his eyes, as if hypnotized, and seemed to lose herself there. He was right. There was no "first" for them.

She had always belonged to him, even before she'd met him. She would belong to him ever after. Always.

DR. FELIX STERNBERGER was at her bedside. He waved two pudgy fingers close to her face.

"How many fingers am I holding up? Carol? Count my fingers."

"Two," she said irritably, and wondered why he wouldn't leave her alone to slip back to her dream of Evan.

"Now how many?"

She squinted, trying to distance herself from the thrusting fingers. "Three."

"Very good. Now, tell me. Are you seeing double? Is your vision abnormal?"

She felt slightly groggy, but her head no longer hurt so viciously, and though her eyes ached, she saw clearly. "Not anymore," she said. "It was bad for a while. It's not now."

He poked her, he prodded her, he nagged her with questions. She answered them dutifully, but with growing resentment.

"Now," he ordered. "Count backward from a hundred."

"No," she snapped. "I already did the damned alphabet again and your multiplication problems. I want my own doctor."

His round face with its foolish walrus mustache was too close to hers; she felt crowded and cornered.

"You'll have to do with me. Do you know how lucky you are that I made a house call? You're being very antagonistic. Hostility is not a good sign. Hostility is a bad sign, a terrible sign. I should put you back in the hospital. I should never have let you leave."

She sank back against the pillow and tried to quell the rebellion in her breast. "I don't want to go to the hospital. I just want to be in my own house—alone."

Charles stood by the door, watching her every move, seeming to hang on her every word. He had changed his fuzzy tan sweater for a heavy blue gray one, the same pale shade as his eyes.

"You're very lucky to have Charles to look after you," Dr. Sternberger said unsympathetically. "Your condition isn't stable, and you need someone with you."

Sternberger straightened and addressed Charles. "You say she's been sleeping too much? Saying irrational things?"

Charles nodded solemnly. "She had me worried. She's had delusions."

"Of what sort?" Sternberger asked.

Charles shrugged and stroked his hand over his balding head. "That her husband's still alive. And about the cat. She seemed to think the cat talks to her."

"What cat?"

Charles stroked his pate again. "She claims she has a cat. But I haven't seen it."

Sternberger turned to her. "Is there really a cat?" he demanded. "Do you know for certain?"

Wariness swarmed through her. "Of course there is. He's keeping to himself because there's a stranger in the house, that's all."

"Could I speak to you in private?" Charles asked, giving Sternberger a look that seemed freighted with meaning.

"Certainly, certainly," Sternberger said, and tweaked the pointed tip of his mustache. He lumbered out to the hall, followed by Charles, who shut the door behind them.

Damn! she thought in irritation. Charles was taking over her house, her life, and he'd talked about her in the third person, as if she were a child. Quietly she rose and padded to the closed door.

She leaned against it, listening. Her head throbbed, but she was better, she could tell.

"... possibility of a subdural hematoma," she heard Sternberger say in his pompous way.

"I'm worried," Charles said. "It's not just the head injury. She hasn't been herself lately. I think she's on the verge of a nervous breakdown."

"Why?"

"She can't let go of her grief for her husband," Charles complained. "I mean, mourning is normal. But for sixteen months? And living in this mausoleum? Now she talks as if she won't sell it."

"Certainly she should sell it," Sternberger agreed. "Depressing place. Unwholesome. Get her out of it, certainly."

"She was restless in her sleep," Charles said, a slight whine in his tone. "She raved on about that cat. She's obsessed with the cat. In fact, I think that's when she started getting odd. When she took in the cat."

"Hmm," mused Sternberger. "I don't like cats myself. Sneaky, slinking beasts."

"This one's particularly sneaky and slinking. I can't even catch sight of the thing. I think it preys on her imagination."

"I supposed it would," Sternberger intoned, "especially in this spooky old tomb of a house."

"She might even be allergic to it," Charles said righteously. "Allergies can affect your nervous system. I read about a man who became violent every time he drank milk."

"Oh, yes," Sternberger concurred. "It's possible, quite possible. I had a similar case. A patient who had headaches and nightmares. Terrible depression. Was sleeping on a goose feather pillow. That was the problem. Foam rubber pillow? No headaches, no nightmares, no depression."

"Exactly," Charles said. "And no matter what, this cat is certainly making her problems worse. I think I should get rid of the thing. If I can lay hands on it. It's not as if she's fond of it. No, it clearly disturbs her."

"I daresay you're right," Sternberger said.

"I think it somehow feeds this sick fantasy that she can get her husband back. I'm sick with pity for her," Charles said. "Just sick. I've got to help her. She can't let this ghost go on haunting her. It's such a waste."

"It is," Sternberger said. "Well, she's got you, and that's a blessing."

"I wonder . . ." Charles said, then hesitated. "I wonder if she shouldn't go for a rest someplace where she could get some good counseling, get herself back on track."

Sternberger whistled softly. "You mean commit her?"

"That's putting it harshly, of course," Charles said. "But . . . I hear shock treatments are coming back, that they can do marvels."

"If she doesn't go voluntarily," Sternberger said somberly, "it's not an easy process."

"She's got no real family to look after her," Charles said. "But as her physician, you could petition the court, couldn't you?"

"Certainly. But it would have to be proved that she was in need of such help. It's a desperate measure."

"I'm only trying to think of every possibility," Charles said.

"I understand."

"But two things are clear to me," Charles said. "I've got to get her out of this house as soon as possible. And get rid of that damned cat."

"Absolutely," Sternberger said. "I couldn't agree more."

She moved away from the door, her pulses drumming, her head aching harder.

I will not leave this house, she thought, clenching her fists. *And if Charles tries to touch the cat, I'll kill him.*

She needed to go to the tower bedroom. It was the gate to Shadowland. And she needed Shadow to take her there, back to Evan. And this time, when she found Evan, she would stay with him.

But as she moved back toward the bed, it occurred to her that anyone who listened to her line of reasoning would think she was completely insane, possibly even self-destructive.

And they would agree with Charles. She should be locked away, given therapy and pills to calm her, shock treatments to burn away her memory.

She sat on the edge of the bed and put her hand to her forehead. *Evan,* she thought desperately, *if you're really there, give me a sign, help me somehow.*

But no sign came. And there was no one to help except, of course, Charles.

Carol had heard that the mad can often be sly. She understood why now. She had to be increasingly sly with Charles.

He'd unplugged the phone in her room and taken it away, so she could rest better, he said. He was intercepting her calls and letting her talk to no one. She shouldn't be disturbed, he'd told her.

He'd arranged, however, for the real estate agent to come to the house that evening so she could sign the sales contract. That, he told her, was something she must do as soon as possible.

Not only had he arranged for her classes to be taught by someone else for the week, he'd canceled his own so that he could take care of her. He'd had someone bring him extra clothing, his toothbrush, his shaving things. He had, in effect, moved in with her.

She was feeling stronger every hour now, but she pretended to be fragile and weak, the better to take him by surprise if the need arose. When she talked to him, she acted politely grateful but cool, and she was careful to sound as calm, rational and cerebral as a professor of logic.

She had devised several plans to get rid of him, and she thought that the best would be the simplest. "I've been thinking," she told him when he brought her supper up to her on a tray.

"Yes?" he asked, and set the tray on her lap.

She stared at it and forced herself to smile, as if pleased. He had microwaved a nasty-looking spaghetti dinner, made a salad of brownish lettuce and filled a dessert dish with something resembling pudding.

He sat down in the chair next to her bed and crossed his legs. "So," he said brightly. "Just what have you been thinking?"

"Oh, lots of things," she said, shaking out the paper napkin. "You're right about the house. I should get out of it. I think I'll go stay with my aunt."

"Your aunt in Elmhurst?" he asked. "But she's ancient, isn't she? You don't have to impose on her. Come to my place. I've got extra room."

"Oh, no," she said. "And my aunt wouldn't mind a bit. But she doesn't like cats. I think I'll give the cat away. I've got a student whose cat was just run over. She's devastated. I'll give her Shadow. He's black, just like hers was."

Charles seemed taken aback, but pleased. "Really? I think that's a wonderful idea. Where is that cat, anyway? I still haven't seen him."

"He keeps to himself," she said casually. "So it's not as if I'll miss his company. Besides, I had nightmares about him when my head was hurting so much. It soured me on him a bit."

"Well," Charles said. "Well, that's very encouraging to hear."

"Yes." She nodded. "I think this whole thing has been fortunate in a way. It's as though I've finally turned the corner. Evan was in my nightmares a lot, too. I suppose it was my way of saying a final goodbye to him."

"Really?" Charles asked. "Carol, that's wonderful. I've been waiting for a long time for you to come back and join the living."

"Absolutely," she agreed. "It's time to get on with life. You've been so incredibly kind and patient. I'm sorry I was sharp with you."

"You were going through a crisis, sweetheart. It was like the crisis of a fever. Now it's over and you're going to be well and whole again."

"Yes, I am," she said confidently. "I can feel it."

"That's wonderful. Now, try to eat something. You've pecked at your food like a bird."

"I'm sorry," she said humbly. "You know I just stopped taking an interest in food for a long time. I don't have much in the kitchen for you to work with. Do you know what I wish I had?"

"What?"

"There's this wonderful little Chinese restaurant down on Main. They make the most wonderful fried dumplings and moo goo gai pan. That's what I'd love. With steamed rice and sweet-and-sour soup."

He leaned toward her and beamed. "If that's what you want, then that's what you'll have. I want my girl to build up her strength."

"Oh, Charles, I couldn't ask you to do that. To go out into the cold. It's snowing again, isn't it?"

"What's snow to a Chicagoan?" he asked. "I wouldn't mind some chow mein myself. You're right. Pickings have been slim. I would have shopped, but I didn't want to leave you."

"You're a prince of a fellow," she said, and gave him a coy smile.

"And you're my princess," he said. He stood, leaned over to take the tray from her and gave her a chaste kiss on the lips.

She forced herself to allow it.

"You're sure you'll be all right?" he asked. "You're still a little shaky on your feet, you know."

"I won't budge from this bed," she vowed. "I'm minding all the doctor's orders now. I want to be completely well as soon as possible."

He smiled so broadly that for a moment she was ashamed of her duplicity, but she coldly fought down any feeling of guilt.

"I'll be back in plenty of time," he said. "The agent isn't coming until eight. Maybe I'll even buy a nice bottle of wine. Then, after you've signed the sale contract, we can have a little celebration. One glass of wine wouldn't hurt you, do you think?"

"It'd probably do me a world of good," she said. "Yes. That's a great idea."

"We'll drink to your new life," he said, beaming.

"Yes," she agreed. "We will."

He turned and left the room. She waited until she heard her front door slam and his car pull away. Then she was out of the bed like a shot and running down the stairs.

She checked the door. He'd locked it, which meant he must have commandeered her keys. She relocked it, shot the bolt, as well and fastened the chain.

Then she padded swiftly to the back door and checked to make sure it was double-bolted against him, too. Then, her heart hammering, she went to the phone and dialed the police station.

Her head was pounding again, and she battled the pain, because she wanted to sound as reasonable and convincing as she could. When an officer answered, she said, "I wish to report a man who's, well, stalking me."

"All right," the man said calmly. "Give me your name, address, the details."

She rattled off her name and address. "I tried to break off our relationship," she said. "He...assaulted me, made me fall down the stairs. When I got out of the hospital, he insinuated his way into my house, and he wouldn't go. He—he even tried to undress me. He won't let me see my own doctor. I've tricked him into leaving for a while. He's gone to the Green Dragon Restaurant on Main Street. I don't want him back here. I don't want him anywhere near me at all."

The voice at the other end of the line sounded almost bored.

"All right, Miz Glendower. I'll have a car dispatched to your place. Don't worry, ma'am."

She hung up the phone. She was trembling, and sweat had broken out on her forehead and in her armpits. She had stretched the truth—but only a bit. It was a terrible thing to do to Charles, an unforgivable one. But there was no way she would let him stand between her and Shadowland.

She picked up the receiver and punched in the phone number of her real estate agent. Her temples throbbed more painfully, and once again she struggled to keep her voice calm and rational.

"Good to hear from you," Hal Gleason said. "I'm glad you're better. I'll be over at eight with the sales agreement. I think we've been very lucky with this."

"No," she said in her most businesslike tone. "Don't bother coming. I didn't make this appointment. Professor Harvey did, and he had no right to. I won't sign anything. I've changed my mind. I'm not selling the house."

There was a moment of stunned silence. When Gleason spoke, his voice was flat and cold. "You can't do that. You listed the house. You signed a contract with us. I have a buyer who is offering you exactly what you asked. You can't violate your contract. It isn't legal."

"I've changed my mind. I won't sell the house. Don't show it anymore. I want my key back or I'll change the locks."

"No," Gleason said, "you don't seem to understand. You can't change your mind. A contract is a contract."

"Contracts can be broken. It happens every day."

"If you do this," he hissed, "I'll see you in court. I'll sue for the commission you've lost me. I'll get it, too."

"Sue away," she said, "if that's what it comes to. This house is not for sale."

"The buyers could take you to court," he warned. "You had a binding agreement to sell the house for a certain price. They offered the price. You're reneging—"

"The house is not for sale, Mr. Gleason. Not at any price. And that's final."

"Dr. Glendower, I don't think you're a well woman. I don't think—"

"I don't really care what you think, Mr. Gleason. Stay away from my house. Goodbye."

She hung up, shaking harder than before. "There. Now I've done it," she whispered to herself. "I've estranged him and Charles, too."

The cat slipped into the room, leaped to the windowsill and sat staring out at the night, into which Charles had disappeared.

"I'm burning my bridges behind me like a maniac," she said. "He's gone, and I won't let him come back. You're so cryptic and so contrary, I suppose you'll tell me now how wonderful he is."

The cat twitched his whiskers in disdain and kept gazing into the darkness. *He? Egregiously an ass.*

She almost laughed. "He made you angry, did he? With all his self-righteous talk of getting rid of you?"

His black tail switched in distaste. *A pestilent, complete knave. The son and heir of a mongrel bitch.*

She smiled in spite of herself. "For once you're making yourself clear. You really don't like him, do you?"

He switched his tail again. *Villain, villain, smiling, damned villain!* His voice was contemptuous. *One may smile and smile and be a villain.*

"You judge him very harshly."

I am nothing if not critical.

Her smile died. "I dreamed of you. You told me to trust you. Not to doubt."

He turned and eyed her coolly. *What's to come is still unsure.* Then he yawned, as if she bored him greatly.

"It wasn't a good dream," she told him, shuddering at the memory. "I dreamed that worms were singing under the stones. They told me that Evan was dead and would never come back. They said you came to deceive me. Were they wrong? Can I trust you?"

He yawned again, showing his sharp white teeth. *You would pluck out the heart of my mystery.* He licked his paw and set to cleaning his whiskers.

She frowned. "They could be right. You might be evil. I've never believed in devils, but—"

He pierced her with a green and icy glare. *Bell, book, and candle shall not drive me back.*

She took a step backward from him. "They used to exorcise demons that way—bell, book, and candle."

His eyes held hers, and he switched his tail more angrily than before. *Bell, book, and candle shall not drive me back.*

Her body had gone stiff with tension and her fists were clenched. "If you're not a figment of my imagination," she

said grimly, "then you're some sort of supernatural creature. But are you good? Or evil?"

Her loud doorbell rasped. It had to be the police, she
realized, her heart giving a frightened leap. Was she really going to do this? Betray Charles for the sake of a cat
and a room haunted by an azure light?

The sound shrilled again, more insistently. The cat laid
back its ears and jumped from the windowsill. He was
running off to hide, as usual.

But he paused long enough to give her one last, taunting look. *The bell invites thee. It is a knell. It summons
thee to heaven—or to hell.*

Then he fled into the shadows and disappeared.

9

A POLICE OFFICER, tall and burly, was at her door. She asked him to come inside. He followed her in, his eyes narrowing thoughtfully at the emptiness of the house.

She wished she'd had time to dress, to brush her hair, put on makeup. She looked wan. But a cunning instinct told her that her appearance could work to her advantage.

She was careful to speak as rationally and clearly as possible to the officer, whose name was McGee. Her head throbbed miserably, but she tried to ignore the pain. Without embellishment she told her story, saying that Charles had practically moved into her house and wouldn't leave.

"He was even going to get rid of my cat behind my back," she finished. "I don't know if he intended to kill it or what."

McGee listened, showing no emotion. "What I can do," he said, "is warn him to stay away, or I'll run him in. But if he continues to harass you, you'll have to get a restraining order against him."

She nodded, a lump in her throat. A restraining order. Charles would never forgive her if it came to that.

She tensed when she heard Charles's car in the driveway. McGee stood, shifted his big shoulders restlessly and went to the door. He turned on the porch light and went outside.

Carol, her heart hammering, watched McGee as he walked down the stairs to Charles's car. Charles stood next to his BMW, his arms full of Chinese food containers. At first his expression was one of bewilderment.

She swallowed hard. He'd gone into the snowy night for her, had faithfully returned, bearing gifts of food. His only sin had been loving her too much, wanting her too desperately.

He shot a glance at the house, and she saw the disbelief and hurt and anger in his face. She had to turn away and not look. He would think her crafty and treacherous, and at this very moment he was probably telling McGee that she was not in her right mind, that she'd had, after all, a serious head injury.

She leaned back against the wall, her eyes still closed. The ache in her temple grew more painful, as if a screw were being twisted more tightly into her skull. But at last she heard Charles's car pulling out of the driveway, and McGee was at the door again.

He didn't come in. He was bearlike in his heavy jacket. He gazed down at her as she shivered at the cold pouring through the open door.

"He says he'll leave you alone," he told her, his face stony. "I'll drive by every hour or so, just to keep an eye on you. If he bothers you again, you'll have to get a restraining order, like I said."

"I understand," she said. She felt chilled by more than the temperature.

He drew one brow down in a frown. "He sounded honestly worried about you. It's obvious you're not feeling good. I'd advise you to get somebody else to stay with you. For your own good, and to keep him at bay. You got somebody?"

"Yes," she lied. "My aunt. She's who I wanted in the first place."

"Good," McGee said. "Get her. Good night, ma'am. Call us if there's any more trouble." He turned and pulled down the brim of his hat more tightly.

"Thank you," she said.

He didn't answer. She watched as he descended the steps again, walked to the black-and-white patrol car that was parked by the curb. He got in and drove away into the night.

She felt frightened and empty, as if she'd crossed some river that divided her from the rest of humanity. She put her hand to her temple, trying to think clearly.

Tomorrow was the day the cat was supposed to take her into Shadowland again, back to Evan. She could tell no one, of course, because anyone who learned the truth would think she was mad.

She had to make certain that nobody tried to interfere with her. She expected Charles to phone at least once. And he would tattle on her—she could think of no other word—telling others that she was not well and was alone, refusing help.

She went to the couch, sat on the arm. She needed another aspirin, but a wave of weakness engulfed her. She knew she should see her own doctor, but how could she leave the house? While she was gone, the gate might open and close again, and she could not risk such a thing.

Her phone rang. She rose and made her way to it, feeling frail and used up. "Hello?" she said, and leaned against the wall to steady herself.

It was Charles. "Don't hang up on me, Carol. Hear me out—please. First of all, I forgive you."

He didn't sound forgiving. He sounded bitter and self-righteous. She sighed in exasperation. Would he never give up, never leave her alone?

"I don't appreciate being lied about," Charles said, his voice tight. "But I don't hold it against you. I know you're not yourself. You're not yourself at all."

"Then who am I?" she asked with weary flippancy. "Leave me alone, Charles. None of this would have happened if you'd only left me alone."

"It is dangerous for you to be alone," he said with sinister emphasis on each word. "You're in the grip of—of fantasies. One such fantasy is that I harassed you, when I was, in truth, only trying to help. But you've had other...aberrational notions, as well. Frankly, Carol, I'm alarmed for your sake."

Her head ached, and she closed her eyes again. "You were going to get rid of my cat," she said from between her teeth. "I heard you talking about it."

"See?" he said triumphantly. "Why bring the cat into it? You obsess about the cat."

"And you seem to obsess about me," she retorted. "Don't you understand? You have no right to move into my house without permission. You have no—"

"You were ill. I did nothing wrong. I slept on the couch. And not very comfortably, either, I might add."

"That's not the point," she said. "You took advantage of my situation to insinuate yourself into my life. I *heard* you, Charles. You even talked about committing me. What gives you the right to—"

"I love you," he said fiercely. "That gives me the right."

"Wrong," she countered. "I know what love is. It's not this awful, meddling possessiveness of yours. I think you're the one who's sick, not me."

"Carol, I will not descend to trading insults with you. You shouldn't be alone. I insist you have someone with you. And if you won't listen to Felix, then I insist you consult a doctor on your own. If you don't—"

"If I don't, then what?" she challenged. "You and your precious Felix will try to get a court order to have me put away?"

"I will do," he said, "whatever needs to be done for your own sake, Carol."

"If you phone me again," she said, "I'll get a restraining order against you. I'll also file a complaint against you with the university. I know you've tried in your way to be kind. But I'm saying goodbye now, Charles. Goodbye. Forever."

"Carol, don't—"

She hung up. Drained, she sank to the floor and sat there, the phone still in her lap. She estimated that Veronica would call in five minutes or less. Charles would be spilling his sad story out to her over the phone at this very moment.

She sat resting, trying to gather strength. *Evan, help me*, she thought. *Let me find my way back to you. Don't let them stop me.*

When the phone rang, she took a deep breath, opened her eyes and answered it. "Hello?"

"Carol, it's Veronica. What in hell is going on over there? Charles says you're alone. I'm coming right over for you. Alvin and I are going to bring you here."

Carol felt as if everything were happening in slow motion, the way one sometimes feels during an accident. Each moment seemed infinitely long, so one could think a multitude of thoughts.

She made her voice as cheery as possible. "Don't be silly. My neighbor's here. Rose Tibbets. I called her right after

I called the police. You've heard me talk about Rose, haven't you?"

"Well, yes," Veronica replied, not sounding convinced.

Rose Tibbets was indeed Carol's neighbor, a retired nurse, the widow of a policeman. But she had left her home last weekend to spend the holidays in Miami with her sister and brother-in-law. Rose Tibbets was more than a thousand miles away. But Veronica didn't know that.

"Rose was a nurse. She'll take fine care of me," Carol said, lying more blithely by the moment. "She said she'd stay until the end of the week, if I needed her."

"Carol, what on earth happened between you and Charles? Why did you call the police, for heaven's sake? He's devastated."

Carol gave a guilty little laugh. "He was horrible, that's what. He wasn't letting me use the phone or anything. He said you called, but he didn't let me talk to you."

"Well, I did phone, of course. More than once," Veronica replied in a musing tone. "But he always said you were resting."

"He took the phone out of my bedroom. He was camping out in my house. He acted as though he'd stay forever. I was starting to feel like the prisoner of love."

"But, honey, the police?"

Carol put her hand to her forehead. She gave another little laugh, more conspiratorial. "Look, it got freaky. He spilled water on me and tried to take my clothes off."

"My God," Veronica said.

"He never called my doctor," Carol went on. "Instead he had that awful Felix Sternberger come over."

"Hmm," Veronica said. "Old Felix was hard to take, I'll give you that."

"Veronica, Charles thought he was going to nurse me through this, and then I'd fall in love with him, and we'd live happily ever after. But he was maddening. He was dictating how I should handle my real estate deal. He was even planning on disposing of my cat."

"Listen, Carol, frankly he said you were getting pretty strange about that cat, and he was worried—"

She closed her eyes against the throbbing in her head. "I had some nightmares, that's all. He blew it all out of proportion. I'm saner than he is. I didn't try to take *his* clothes off."

"Now, what you're saying," Veronica replied, "is old Charles has a bit of a perverse streak?"

Carol began to lie. Her lies might be found out eventually, but at this point, it was her word against Charles's. "Yes. He—he groped me a couple of times in my sleep. He said he was trying to wake me up because I was having nightmares. Veronica, I was truly scared that he was going to force himself on me."

"Charles?" she asked dubiously.

"Charles," Carol insisted, embroidering the truth. "It started Tuesday when he came over. He wouldn't leave. He said he'd been too much of a wimp, and now he was going to be macho. Forceful. I don't know—he must have thought he was going into Rhett Butler mode. He—he made a pass."

"Charles as Rhett Butler?" Veronica asked, even more doubtfully.

"It's the truth," Carol vowed. "I tried to tell you in the hospital. He literally pursued me up the stairs. Then when I fell, he moved himself in here and appointed himself my guardian. It was scary. I felt like the heroine in a Gothic novel."

"Carol, you're not kidding me, are you?"

"How long have you known me?"

"Four years."

"Have I ever, that you know of, lied to you in those four years?"

"No," Veronica said, almost reluctantly.

"Do I sound sane to you. Or am I coming across like a raving maniac?"

"All right. You sound sane. And come to think of it, Charles was the one who sounded, well, distraught. But, Carol?"

"Yes?"

"You did bang your head. It did knock you out. And you were saying mighty weird things. Charles is afraid that you won't see a doctor. Does your head still hurt?"

"Hardly at all," Carol fibbed.

"Will you see a doctor?"

"I'll call one right now," Carol said, proud of her ingenuity. "My friend, Jerry Bratling. You know, the guy from grad school days. He's a psychiatrist, and he ought to be able to tell you if I'm bonkers. How's that?"

Veronica was silent a moment. "How's a psychiatrist going to help you with a banged head?"

"Because psychiatrists have to go to medical school first. Psychologists don't. That's the difference. Jerry can handle a bump on the head, no problem."

"You'll have him call me?"

"I promise. If I can get him. If I can't, I'll have Rose take me to my regular doctor first thing in the morning."

Veronica sounded reluctant. "All right. Then let me talk to what's her name. Rose Tibbets. Just so I'll know somebody's with you."

"She's at the convenience store, getting groceries," Carol lied. "That's how I got Charles out of the house. There's nothing to eat here. But she'll be back. Would I deceive you?"

"I hope not," said Veronica. "If I haven't heard from your doctor tonight, I'm calling you again in the morning. I can be a nag, in case you haven't noticed."

Carol smiled weakly. "I've noticed."

"I've got a mind to send Alvin over there to check on you."

"Keep him home," Carol said lightly. "By the time he got here from the city, all he'd find is two cranky women who want to go to bed. It's cold out. Keep him where it's warm."

At last Veronica agreed. Carol told her good-night and hung up the phone. Perspiration filmed her forehead, and the blood banged in her temples.

"Aspirin," she said. Painfully she rose and hobbled into the downstairs bathroom. She took four aspirin, washed her face, brushed her hair and put on a touch of makeup.

Then she made her way to the laundry room. She took off the rumpled flannel pajamas and put on a pair of freshly ironed jeans and a sweatshirt with a design of hollyberries on it.

After slipping on a pair of slipper socks, she went to the kitchen and made herself a cup of tea and a bowl of microwave oatmeal. By the time she finished, her head hurt less. She went back to the bathroom and brushed her teeth.

She studied herself in the mirror. Her red gold curls sparkled like fire, and although she was pale, she looked surprisingly normal. Not in the least like a woman preparing to go on a supernatural journey.

It crossed her mind that if she went into the blue light, she might not return. Her mouth went dry, and it hurt to swallow. Perhaps she really had said goodbye to Charles forever, and Veronica, too.

Perhaps she was saying goodbye to everyone and everything she knew. And venturing into what? Exile?

I won't think that, she told herself. *All I'll think of is that I'm going to Evan.*

She lifted her chin defiantly and went back to the living room and picked up the phone again. She dialed Jerry Bratling's number. This was the boldest and most dangerous part of her plan.

JERRY APPEARED on her doorstep within an hour. Snow was falling again, and flakes were caught in his bushy hair. His lanky body was bundled up in the thickest parka she had ever seen. It looked as if it had been pumped up with air.

"I didn't want you to come," she told him, letting him in. But she had known he would come. He was that kind of friend.

He shucked off the enormous parka, unwound his muffler. He frowned at her in concern. "Carol, I called this Dr. Sternberger. He took this head injury much more seriously than you. He said your symptoms indicate that you might have some internal swelling."

"What symptoms?" she asked airily. She led him into the kitchen and gestured for him to sit at the table. While waiting for him, she'd made coffee, and she poured them each a cup.

"Double vision," Jerry said, studying her solemnly. "Drowsiness. Irrational talk. Even personality changes."

"Jerry," she said, sitting down across from him and staring him in the eye, "Felix Sternberger is an alarmist. It's true I had some vision problems and sleepiness at first. But that's over. As for irrational talk, I had some dreams, that's all."

Jerry took off his thick glasses, polished them on the napkin. "He mentioned you were talking about the cat. About Evan not being dead. Are those thoughts persisting?"

He put the glasses back on and stared at her. He was not going to be easy to fool, but she must fool him.

She laughed, just a little. "If I said anything about that ridiculous business, it's because it was fresh in my mind. No, you were absolutely right. That whole episode was an elaborate fantasy. To avoid the truth."

His homely face was stern, but kindly. "And what's the truth, Carol?"

She let her smile fade into an expression of sadness. Once more, she met his eyes. "The truth is that Evan is dead. What's over is over. And it's time to get on with my life."

Jerry sipped his coffee, then shook his head. "Tell me this. Do you think getting on with your life means throwing your boyfriend out the door and threatening him with a restraining order?"

She took a deep breath and cocked her head thoughtfully. She kept her voice calm. "He wasn't my boyfriend, and he wasn't willing to accept that. This whole silly thing was brought on because I'd met another man, remember? Charles refused to accept that."

"So you went from the frying pan into the fire, eh?" he asked. "From one crisis into another?"

"Is that so unusual?" she asked. "If I'd been in a healthier frame of mind in the first place, I wouldn't have gotten involved with Charles. I fell into a completely neurotic relationship without realizing it."

Jerry sighed and tipped back in his chair, balancing it on two legs. "Bingo, kid. That's exactly how it works. I've seen it too often."

"So why be concerned?" she asked matter-of-factly. "He wasn't exactly playing fair with me. Felix Sternberger is his cousin, Jerry. I felt the two of them were ganging up on me when I was down."

"Okay," Jerry said, just as matter-of-factly. "Sternberger said Charles phoned him, upset. Really upset that you'd called the police. Do you think you overreacted?"

She spread out her hands, palm up. "If you were in my position, stuck in a house with a man who wouldn't take no for an answer, what would you do? If he'd actually moved in with you, unasked? If he'd taken the phone away and wouldn't let you talk to anybody else?"

"Sternberger seemed to think Charles was just doing his job. Out of concern."

"Sternberger would," she said, with the slightest edge of contempt. "I didn't choose him either, you know."

"And your friend Veronica—she's concerned," Jerry said. "She doesn't want you staying alone."

"I'm not alone," Carol lied. "My neighbor's here, Mrs. Tibbets." She nodded toward the back door and held her breath.

After she'd called Jerry, she'd put on an old pair of snow boots and an ancient jacket and trudged back and forth between her house and Rose's several times. She'd put the snow boots on the mat beside the back door, hung the snowy jacket over a chair to dry.

She'd promised to pick up Mrs. Tibbets's mail while she was in Florida, and she'd set two of her magazines on the kitchen table, as if she'd been browsing through them.

She'd made another cup of tea and poured it out, so there were now two teacups in the sink, as though she'd had a guest.

Jerry eyed the wet snow boots by the door and the jacket on the chair. He picked up one of the magazines and noted

Rose's name on the address label. "And this Mrs. Tibbets is upstairs, asleep?" he asked.

"Yes," Carol said. "She's an early bird. Do you want me to go wake her?"

"No, no," Jerry said wearily. "I believe you. Tell me—how are you feeling physically?"

"A little shaky," she answered. "A little headachy. Otherwise, fine. Except not sleepy. I napped enough for two people yesterday."

"Okay," he said. "Let me shine the light in your eyes, do the whole bit."

"Fine," she said with resignation. "Just please don't ask me to recite the alphabet again. I can probably say it backward at this point."

He shone the light in her eyes, and she prayed that her pupils were the same size, their appearance normal.

"Hmm," Jerry said noncommittally. He had her walk for him, balance on one foot, do exercises in hand coordination.

"Hmm," he said again, and scratched his head.

"Well?" she asked.

"Your pupils look fine. Your reactions are a little slow, a little tentative. That's all. But you should be careful."

"Careful?"

"Head injuries are tricky, Carol. You might go along a week, two weeks, before the complications really hit you. Sternberger's right about that. You should have somebody keeping an eye on you."

"I do," she said innocently. "Rose. She said she'd stay over a few nights, then look in on me from time to time."

"Sure you wouldn't want to come back home with me?" he offered. "You could stay with Carmen and me. We've got a guest room."

"With Rose already here?" she asked. "I wouldn't think of it. Carmen has enough on her mind with another baby coming. I wouldn't have called you away from her tonight, but—"

"But you didn't want your friends thinking you were loco for giving the boot to the all-too-ardent Charles?"

She looked away, embarrassed. "Well, we do have mutual friends. And he'd called one and really frightened her. Honestly, Jerry, you've known me forever. Would I have phoned the police if I could have thought of anything else to do?"

He raised and lowered his heavy eyebrows in a sort of shrug. "I *have* known you forever, kid. And you sound as sane as you always did. But like I said, I want you to be careful."

"In what way?"

"Come see me on Friday at two," he said. "I can work you in. Take it easy. Rest as much as you can. Let this Mrs. Tibbets do her stuff."

"Absolutely," she vowed.

"If you—or she—sees any change in you, call me immediately, understand?"

"I understand."

"And Carol, listen. If you should have any more thoughts or dreams or visions about Evan not being dead, get in touch with me right away. Understand?"

"Yes."

He smiled at her rather sadly. "The cat hasn't led you to an alternate universe again, has he?"

She forced herself to laugh. "No. He's been completely earthbound."

"Sternberger told me that Charles claims you think the cat talks to you."

She laughed even more ironically. "In a dream, Jerry. The cat talked to me in a dream."

"What did he say?" he asked.

The question took her by surprise. She frowned slightly. "I really can't remember," she lied. "You know dreams. They fade."

He glanced around the kitchen. "Where is this fabled cat, by the way?"

"Who knows?" she said lightly. "He hides whenever a stranger comes. He hid as soon as Rose showed up. Do you know a good psychiatrist for cats?"

"I'm sure there's one out there somewhere," he said sardonically. "All right, Carol. I'll call your friend and tell her that you seem to be in good shape. But take care."

"I will," she promised. Her deceit had worked, and her spirits were high. Her pulses pounded, and she tried hard to disguise her excitement.

"For instance," he said, almost casually, "don't make any big decisions right now. You know? You're still in an iffy stage. So no big life and death choices, okay?"

The words shook her, but she kept her calm facade. "No life and death choices," she promised, smiling coolly.

But that's exactly what she feared she was about to make.

Carol knew Jerry still had reservations about calling Veronica, but he did it anyway. In a resigned voice, he said that Carol's condition seemed good, she was quite rational and a neighbor was staying with her.

When he bade Carol goodbye, he squeezed her hand affectionately and said he'd see her on Friday.

She agreed heartily.

When she closed the door behind him, she leaned against it, worn out by her charade. When she heard his car start, then back out of the driveway, she began crying.

Jerry was one of her oldest friends, and she had lied to him and used him shamelessly. She realized that if she went to Evan, she would probably never see Jerry again, either. Or Carmen. Or Brian, their little boy. She would never see their new baby, or know if it was a boy or girl.

Suddenly she was overwhelmed by all the people, all the things she would miss. And for what was she trading these things that she loved? For an unknown. A total unknown. In the hope of regaining Evan. Not for the promise of regaining him. Only the slim and chancy hope.

She cried harder.

She sensed, rather than saw, that the cat had come into the room.

"You," she said, turning to him resentfully. "I don't even know where you'll lead me. Where is Evan, dammit?"

Aloofly the cat looked her up and down. It occurred to her that black cats were witch's cats, Satanic cats, and that superstition had equated them with evil for centuries.

"Where's Evan?" she demanded, her voice tearful. "Where?"

The cat did not blink. His voice came into her mind cold and mocking. *He is dead and gone, lady. He is dead and gone.*

She jerked upright and glared at him. "How can you say that? I've seen him. Where will I be if I go with him?"

He switched his tail in his slow, contemptuous way. *Play out the play.*

She clenched her fist against the door. "I said, where will I be if I go to him? What becomes of me?"

He laid back his ears slightly, as if impatient. *Play out the play.*

"You devil," she accused. "This isn't fair. Give me some hint. What happens if I go to him? Am I dead, too?"

He turned his head, gazed off into the shadows, as if they held more interest for him than she did. The voice echoed ominously in her mind again. *Play out the play.*

"Why are you doing this to me?" She hurled the words at him. "Why are you torturing me like this?"

He moved away so smoothly that his bell made no sound. He gave her one last, impenetrable, green glance.

I must be cruel, only to be kind.

"Is that true?" she asked desperately. "Will you be kind? Can I trust you—as you said in my dream?"

A dream itself is but a shadow.

"You know what I mean," she begged. "In the end you won't mislead me? Can I trust you? Or can't I?"

I am myself indifferent honest, he said in his haughty, weary way.

Then he slipped away into the darkness.

10

CAROL TOOK two more aspirin and made her way to bed. She feared that her nerves were too tattered for sleep, but sleep came. At first she dreamed of Evan, again as if she were reliving the experience with perfect accuracy.

They were camping in Tanzania, high on the crest of the volcano. The volcano had been inactive for centuries, and scientists said it would never erupt again. Yet Carol thought it wrong to call the volcano dead, for it was host to so much life.

The rich volcanic earth sprouted lush grasses, a wealth of wildflowers and exotic trees. Below, the rolling savanna teemed with wildlife, and a herd of elephants grazed, bathed in the crooked river and tended their young.

Evan had friends, a couple named DeBerg, who were wildlife photographers and had permission to follow the herd, which was protected by the government. The DeBergs had invited Evan and Carol to join them for the weekend and said it was all right for them to hike to the crater of the volcano and camp.

The DeBergs trusted Evan to keep out of trouble and respect the environment. They had smiled a bit indulgently at Evan and Carol, the smile of people amused by seeing a young couple obviously in love.

The DeBergs' trust in Evan was merited. He was an excellent outdoorsman, so knowledgeable and at ease in the wild that Carol had laughed and nicknamed him Tarzan.

They stopped halfway up the slope that afternoon and watched the elephants from that vantage point. The herd was scattered among the trees, feeding, and a mother and calf were taking a mud bath at the river's edge.

Evan could name most of the plants and animals they saw, even the insects. Africa produced a prodigious number of insects, and Carol admired them with scientific interest, although deep down they made her uneasy. Evan knew this, but didn't tease her.

He found a recently dead hummingbird, a beautiful creature, green and gold and rosy red. It was the largest hummingbird she'd ever seen, and she was saddened by its still, gleaming body.

"What do you suppose happened to it?" she asked Evan. "There's not a mark on it."

He shook his head. "Nature's full of mysteries, love. But look—there's a pair of live ones."

She gazed in the direction of his pointing finger and saw two of the iridescent birds, hovering and darting among a stand of trumpet-shaped orange flowers.

They watched the birds for a long time, then continued their hike to the top. Evan set up a simple camp, built a fire, and together they made supper. As simple as the food was, it was delicious after the long climb.

When night fell, the sky was velvety blue and spangled with uncountable stars. He pointed out the constellations they wouldn't be able to see when they were back home in North America. The half-moon hung low, huge and pocked and silvery blue.

They sat looking up at the sky, Evan with his arm around her, she with her head on his shoulder.

"Know what I like about camping?" he asked in a lazy voice.

"What?" she said, just as lazily.

"Nothing to do after the sun goes down. Except stare at the sky awhile, then go to bed."

"Bed?" she asked innocently.

"Bed," he said with conviction. He gazed up at the star-strewn sky again. He shook his head. "It's so untouched here. I feel like we're in Eden."

"Yes," she said, and nuzzled the strong, warm column of his neck.

He turned to her, putting his hands on her shoulders. "Except," he drawled, "Eve didn't have all these pesky clothes."

"Oh?" she said a bit breathlessly. "Well, you're a man of action. Do something about it."

His hands moved to the top button of her camp shirt. "I never," he said, "turn down a challenge."

With maddening slowness, as if enjoying the rising suspense of desire, he undid the buttons, one by one. She watched him, her heart beating as hard as the wings of one of the hummingbirds in flight.

The moon and stars were so bright she could see everything clearly, even the little white scar that ran across the base of his knuckle. His silver ID bracelet glinted in the moonlight; his wedding ring winked.

His wavy hair, too long as usual, fell across his brow, shadowing it. The blue glow of the moon cast the shadow of his long lashes on his cheekbones, limned the sculpted lines of his lips. When he raised his eyes to hers, they seemed a more lively and intense blue than the gleaming sky.

She gasped involuntarily. He had always been handsome, but at that moment he looked positively beautiful to her. She thought fleetingly of the Greek myth about the young man who had been so beautiful that the goddess of the moon had fallen in love with him.

"What's wrong?" he asked, frowning slightly in concern.

"Nothing," she said tightly. "It's just you look so wonderful in the moonlight."

He gave her his special half smile. "No," he said. "You're the one who looks wonderful."

Gently he drew back the halves of her unbuttoned shirt, dropping his gaze to her breasts. The moon and starshine tinted her white bra to blue. He lowered the shirt from her shoulders, slid it from her arms.

Silently the shirt fell to the sleeping bag on which they sat. Then his lean hands undid the front fastening of her bra. With a delicate click it came undone.

With the same gentleness he drew off her bra, so that her breasts were naked of everything except moonlight. The bra, too, slid to the sleeping bag. He put his hands on her bare shoulders and stared at her pale breasts.

"My God," he whispered, "you *are* beautiful."

He lowered his face and kissed first one tender nipple, then the other. Then he laved each with his tongue and kissed them again. With controlled urgency he suckled them until their points swelled and hardened with pleasure.

His hands moved to hold and caress them as his mouth made love to them. She laced her fingers in his thick hair and drew him even closer. "Evan," she begged raggedly, "stop. You're going to make me climax before we even—"

"Go ahead," he murmured. "I love you. I want it to happen more than once for you."

She half sighed, half moaned. Her breasts felt full of fiery liquor, and the more he sucked and kissed, the more strongly it seemed to flow. It coursed downward to the center of her femininity, an irresistible flood of need and heat.

His hands, his mouth did magical, maddening things to her, and the inner rivers of desire surged higher and deeper and hotter.

"I want you inside me," she begged, her voice broken. She wanted to feel his naked skin, feel his weight, his heavenly hard thrust into her softness and wetness.

"No," he said. "Not yet. It's all right, love. Just let it happen."

She gave herself completely to his seduction of her breasts. She let it happen. She felt herself turning into a bright swirl of desire, and the swirl overwhelmed her, became the only thing in the universe.

The swirl was her; it was Evan; it was love commingled with desire so intense that she was swept away, riding its strong, tidal pulsing. Her mind went momentarily dark. She turned into pure, euphoric sensation.

It shook through her, and when it subsided, she still trembled weakly. "Oh, Evan," she said in a shaking voice. "Oh. Oh, my."

"No," he said, pushing her back gently so that she lay on the sleeping bag. "Oh, mine. You're mine, and I'm yours. Any pleasure I give you is mine, too. Let it happen again. I want to love you all over."

He was unsnapping her shorts, drawing them down and freeing her from them. Then he did the same thing with her panties. He began to stroke her thighs, kiss her stomach, trailing his kisses lower, making her vibrate with need again.

A second time he turned her into a vortex of sparkling desire. She imagined that they were at the center of some new galaxy that was whirling into bright, explosive being. Again she was breathless, limp.

She lay back against the sleeping bag. He sat up, unbuttoned his shirt and cast it away. He pulled off his few remaining clothes and sat naked in the starlight. He stared down at her, trailing a finger along her jaw.

"They say the third time's the charm," he teased, but his voice was husky with yearning for her.

She gazed up at him, faint with love. The stars seemed to dance around his head, and the moonlight gleamed on his naked shoulders. "I want to do for you what you've done for me," she said softly.

She took him to the edge of his control and almost beyond. When he finally wrapped her in his arms and laid her down again, his voice with thick with need. "It's going to be fast, honey. I'm sorry. I just can't hold back any longer."

She didn't care. She wanted him as much as he wanted her. When he entered her, she shuddered with pleasure, and that was all it took, the feel of him inside her, to set her off again in sweet, mind-blinding spasms.

They lay holding each other tightly, kissing each other deeply. Afterward they'd climbed into the sleeping bag and held each other all night long. She had never imagined being this happy. She had not known it was possible.

At dawn they awoke to find the volcano's peak lost in a sea of white clouds. Nearby there was the drowsy twitter of birds. Far below them, the elephants trumpeted, welcoming the dawn.

But up there, at the crater's grassy edge, the dawn was only that unreal, soft whiteness. They might have been lying in heaven, so pure was the white, so coolly pleasant was its still air.

"What is it?" she breathed against Evan's neck, holding him more tightly. "Fog?"

"Clouds, love," he said, his lips close to her ear. "We're in the clouds."

She laughed softly, delighted by the thought. If she closed her eyes, all she saw was darkness. If she opened them, all she saw was the shifting, silvery white. And from the river came the haunting cry of the elephants calling to one another.

"It's like magic," she said. "It's like waking to the first morning of the world."

"It is," he murmured.

He held her in silence for a long moment, his naked body warm against hers.

Then he kissed her ear and said, "Last night we played around so much that I went off too fast. How about if I try to do it very, very slo-owly. Or are you worn out?"

It was the morning of the world, and she loved him so extravagantly that she felt she could never weary of it. "Oh, Evan," she said, nestling closer to him, "maybe this really *is* heaven." Then she laughed softly, because without meaning to, she'd made a rhyme: Evan, heaven.

"Maybe it is," he answered, and unzipped the sleeping bag. They made love on top of it again, their only covering the clouds.

SHE AWOKE ABRUPTLY in what seemed to be the middle of the night. The black cat was sitting on her chest. The glow from the night-light made his green eyes glint.

She was suddenly frightened without knowing why. She stole a glance at the digital clock. It was half past one in the morning.

"What is it?" she asked warily.

The cat gave her a languidly slow blink. *There be souls must be saved*, said the weary, aloof voice. *And there be souls must not be saved.*

She recoiled. The cat rose, shuddered daintily and stepped from her chest. He stood a foot or so farther away and eyed her coldly.

"What's that supposed to mean?" she asked, her heart racing. "There are souls that must be saved and souls that mustn't?"

There was no answer. The cat simply stared at her in his unnerving way.

A few webs of sleep had clung to her. They dissolved and fell away when a realization pierced her consciousness. "The gate?" she asked, apprehension rising. "Is it open? The light? Is it back? Have you come to take me to Evan?"

Another slow and haughty blink. *Journey's end in lovers' meeting.*

He turned and leaped softly from the bed. His bell gave the faintest jingle. He cast one unreadable glance at her, then walked silently to the door.

She glanced at the clock again, her throat tightening in fear. If it was past midnight, then it was Thursday, and it was three days since she'd been to Shadowland. Perhaps it was already time.

Quickly she slipped from bed. She didn't bother to put on slippers or robe, although the house was chilly. She wore only a simple white nightgown.

Her head still ached, and once again she felt slightly nauseated, but she hurried after the cat, who had crept out the door. She switched on the hall light just in time to see him steal inside the tower bedroom. Its door, closed when she'd gone to bed, was slightly ajar now.

She ran down the hall, threw open the door. Her blood seemed to stop flowing; her heart felt paralyzed. She could only stare for a moment.

Where the bed had stood, there was now a huge, jagged column of motionless blue light. It was of no real shape, yet it had edges. Its angles made her think of a huge, live crystal made of light.

The bed was either hidden or gone; it was as if the light had devoured it. The cat stood, a black silhouette against the azure. He looked toward her, as if he'd been waiting for her.

She trembled. Her temple throbbed unmercifully. What had Jerry warned? To make no big decision at this time, no life and death choice.

The cat switched his dark tail as if in impatience. Perhaps he sensed her hesitation.

She clutched the doorframe as if assuring herself of its reality. She couldn't take her eyes from the eerie column of light that dominated the center of the room, floor to ceiling.

"Where does it go?" she whispered. "What am I setting out for—really?"

The voice almost hissed in her mind. *Life's uncertain voyage.*

"Uncertain," she echoed unhappily. Everything had been uncertain from the time she had first followed the cat to this room.

All that was sane fairly shrieked at her that this was impossible. Her friends had warned her that she was not thinking clearly, and to make matters worse, she had hurt her head. Her usually trusty brain, so logical, so keen, might be tricking her.

She had cast aside a faithful suitor and done it brutally. She had dissembled to doctors and lied to friends. Her very dreams had warned her that trying to follow after Evan was a kind of death.

The cat switched his tail again, the motion clearly angry. *Nothing will come of nothing,* the voice in her mind warned, its tone ominous. The cat stepped into the light and disappeared.

His words echoed in her mind, haunting her: *"Nothing will come of nothing."* Nothing ventured, nothing gained. She took a deep breath and walked to the azure glow.

"I loved you, Evan," she breathed, and stepped into the thick pillar of silent light.

She was in Evan's arms. It was not a dream. He was real; she was sure.

The arms that held her were vital with working muscle, warm with life. The lips that moved so hungrily upon her own were his. Beneath her hands, she felt the familiar contours of his strong body.

"I love you," he kept saying between kisses, his voice tense with emotion.

It was Evan's familiar low voice, and his breath warmed her cold lips. Even his scent, of bay rum, was right and exciting.

She kissed him back and clung to him as tightly as she could. At last he drew back to look down into her eyes. She realized that her face was wet with tears.

His beautiful blue eyes were troubled. He wiped away a tear with his thumb.

"I was afraid you wouldn't come," he said, his voice taut. "And I was afraid you would."

"Evan, I've had such dreams. It was as if we were really together in Africa again. I've never had such dreams."

He wiped away another tear, the set of his mouth somber. "I think They've made that happen."

She shook her head. "But I had a nightmare, too. The worst I've ever had. Worms told me you were dead."

"I think They made that happen, as well."

"But why?" she asked, holding on to him more fiercely. This time she didn't want to be forced to let him go. Not now, not ever.

"I think they're testing us."

She raised her hand and touched the familiar curve of his cheekbone. "Why? Why is this happening?"

His hands were on her upper arms, and his gaze moved up and down her body, full of perplexity and desire. "All They've said is 'Sometimes, if you love enough . . .'"

Her heart wrenched painfully. She tried to smooth his unruly forelock back from his brow, but stubbornly, as of old, it fell back again. "Sometimes, if you love enough— what?" she pleaded.

His eyes rested on hers again, looking more pained than before. "I don't know. That's all They'll say. 'Sometimes, if you love enough . . .'"

"That's why the light came? That's why They opened a door in time and space?"

He stared at her face as if memorizing it before he had to go away. "I think maybe it means, if you love somebody enough, you can be damned."

She blinked in shock. Her body went rigid, and her throat tightened. "Damned? What do you mean?"

"I mean I couldn't let you go, even in death. It didn't matter what was on this side. I wanted you."

"I wanted you, too. More than anything."

He frowned and shook his head. "You shouldn't love me more than life. Or than your soul. It's wrong. They're tempting you. You've got to let go. We both have to."

"No," she cried stubbornly, and fresh tears streaked her cheeks.

"Carol. Carol, listen," he said. "The gate's going to close soon. They're sending me away. I don't know where. Or to what."

"I'll go with you," she vowed.

"No," he said, and swallowed hard. "I can't let you. It might be to real death. To nothingness. It might be...something worse."

"What's worse than being without you?"

He searched her face. "Maybe being trapped with me, hating me for what I'd led you into. And this time there'd be no escape. I can't chance that, Carol. I love you too much."

"But—but," she said, nearly overcome with emotion, "you said that They told you *I* had to choose."

"We both have to choose," he said, gripping her arms. "And I want you to choose life as you know it. It's what I want for you. A real life. A husband. Children—"

"I don't want anybody's children but yours," she said desperately. "And how do you know they'd send us someplace bad? It might be wonderful. It would be, if you were there."

"Love, I can promise you nothing," he told her. "*Nothing*. Not comfort, not safety, not even existence."

"Half the time I wish I'd stayed in Africa with you," she said, her voice full of bitterness. "So the fever had taken me, too."

"No," he said earnestly. "Never think that way. It's wrong. Don't you see? It's like a temptation. You've got to choose to stay there next time. On the other side."

"The next time?" she asked in despair. "You mean I have to go back again?"

He traced the line of her eyebrow. "Yes. The gate will open one more time. It's like the last tempting for you. You've got to resist. Stay. Live a good life. Do it for me."

"Evan," she pleaded, "I can't go back there. I can't leave you again. I couldn't stand it."

"You have to," he said, his face grim. "Or They'll take it out on me again. And maybe this time on you, too. You've seen that They aren't all benevolence. They can cause pain. A lot of it."

"Evan, this is terrible," she said. "It's like losing you twice. Why is this happening?"

"I think I lost my soul for loving you," he said. "I don't want the same thing happening to you. Go back. Stay back, so They don't get you, too."

"Don't confuse me," she begged. "The cat—he talks to me, inside my head, the way you say They talk to you. And everything he says is crooked and twisted, and I don't know what to believe and what not—"

"Believe me. Go back. Stay back. Find someone to love you. It'll be easy. You're so easy to love. You want children. Have them."

"Only with you," she protested. "Only with you."

"I can't promise you that," he said. "And I think the cat is doing exactly what They want him to do. Confuse you. Make you conscious that there *is* a choice. And there's danger."

"Is he one of Them?" she asked. "In my nightmare, worms talked. They said he was—was like a devil."

"He's not one of Them. I know that much. He's some sort of messenger. Or maybe a tempter. Maybe that's why he's a black cat. As an omen. That he can lead you into evil."

"Maybe it's to throw me off track," she countered. "Maybe it's to frighten me and to test my nerve. Even to doubt my sanity."

"He's at home over here," Evan said, frowning again. "But he's restless. He—"

They heard a distant but strong "Meow," and they both heard it at once. Both turned and looked off into the infinite blueness. Far away in the featureless glow, they saw the cat's black shape loping smoothly toward them.

Carol blinked back her tears, her eyes burning. The cat bounded through luminous space as if it provided a floor beneath his paws. His gait was almost joyful, unlike any motion she'd ever seen him make in her world.

"He's got something in his mouth," Evan said, narrowing his eyes. His tone was apprehensive. "I wish I'd never sent the bracelet to you with the devil."

"I—I don't believe he's a devil," Carol said hesitantly. "I believe he's come to help us."

"So did I," Evan said, gripping her more protectively. "At first."

The cat ran up to them, and he was indeed carrying something in his mouth. He opened his jaws, and the object dropped soundlessly at their feet.

She saw what it was and gasped as Even picked it up. He straightened, holding it in the palm of his hand. It was a dead bird.

But what shook her was that it was not an ordinary bird; it was as large a hummingbird as she'd ever seen. It was an African hummingbird, the sort she and Even had seen on the climb up the volcano.

Even in the blue light, she could see its rich colors, the iridescent gold and green and ruby. It might have been the very bird they had found that day.

"Oh, my God," she said, putting her hand to her mouth. "It's from Africa. Evan, the cat's been to Africa. He must have been. Maybe it's a hint of where They'd send us. Africa. Or someplace like it."

"No," Evan said, stone faced. "It could be a trick."

"Meow," said the cat, and rubbed affectionately against her ankles. "Meow." He began to purr loudly.

"But it doesn't have to be a trick," she said, putting her hand on Evan's arm. "It might even be a promise."

"And it might be a warning," he said between his teeth. "Look at it, Carol. It's dead. In this place, I'm whole, I'm live, but it's dead. Maybe that's what's waiting for me. And that's why you can't come."

The cat rubbed more sensuously against her, purred even more loudly, a rhythmic thrumming noise. Evan cast him a cold look, but then winced as if in pain.

"They want you to go," he said. "I do, too. They'll give you one more chance to come back. Don't take it."

"Evan," she said, panic rising, "are they hurting you again?"

He let the bird fall from his hand. It lay at their feet, seeming to rest on sheer light and nothingness. "Kiss me goodbye," Evan said, seizing her. He pulled her to him almost roughly. "Always remember that I love you," he said. "And that I want you to have a good life, a full life, a happy life. Goodbye, Carol."

She started to protest, but his mouth bore down on hers, and he kissed her with such hungry passion and despair that she could only answer him in kind.

Their mouths fused, as if they would devour each other, and they held each other as tightly as they could. She couldn't breathe, but she didn't care. She wished she could be pressed against him hard enough to become one with him, so they could never be unjoined again.

But then he drew back with a sound deep in his throat, almost like a sob of pain. "Now. They say to go—now."

He stepped backward, almost involuntarily, then he doubled up and a strangled groan escaped him. He swore. His body twisted in agony.

"No!" she cried. "I love you, Evan." But she turned and fled, for his sake. The cat bounded before her, leading the way.

The next thing she knew, she was lying prone on the floor of the tower bedroom. She was panting, and her heart hammered as if she had just run a long way. Her face was still wet with tears.

She pushed herself to a sitting position and looked at the bed. It sat on its dais, its usual massive self, slightly dusty, covered with the fading fringed throw. The only light in the room came streaming through at the edges of the ragged blinds.

The cat sat on the bed like a king seated on his throne. He licked his paw, his eyes closed in concentration. Flick, flick, flick went his pink tongue.

"Is Evan right?" she asked, her voice shaking with bitterness. "Are you some kind of devil?"

Flick, flick went the tongue against the black paw. Somehow the closed eyes made his expression seem almost blissful. *Can the devil speak true?*

"What sort of thing are you really?" she demanded.

He laid back his ears, looking even more ecstatic. *My kind? Why, we are what we are. Gentlemen of the shade, minions of the moon.*

"I think you're no gentleman," she said between clenched teeth.

The prince of darkness is a gentleman.

"When does the gate open again?" she asked him. "When?"

Night, said the cool, bored voice.

"This night? Tonight?"

He ceased his washing, opened his green eyes. *Tonight. My dearest love, tonight.*

He rose, stretched lazily, then leaped from the bed and ambled to the open door. She stared after him, her heart still beating hard. "Shadow!" she cried.

He stopped and stared at her as if affronted.

"They hurt him again. They can hurt as well as heal. Is he right? If I go to him, will we both be damned?"

The pale eyes blinked slowly. He stared through her. *Some rise by sin and some by virtue fall.*

He padded soundlessly out the door, leaving her sitting on the bare, dusty floor. She wiped the back of her hand across her mouth, pushed a red gold strand of hair out of her eyes.

"'Some rise by sin,'" she whispered to herself, "'and some by virtue fall.'"

She swallowed and wearily rose to her feet. It seemed she had been in Shadowland only moments, but again she'd lost another complete night. The sunlight falling through the windows looked strong enough to be noon light.

She put her fingertips to her temple. Her headache was gone, she could not even feel the tenderness of the bruise any longer. She crossed the room, peered into the cloudy mirror that leaned against the wall.

She pushed her hair back from her face and held it there. The bruise had vanished. Even the small cut had disappeared, healed completely.

She straightened and went to the door, stepped into the hall. The cat sat in the middle of the hallway rug. He eyed her haughtily.

"This is torture, you know," she said, narrowing her eyes at him. "Sheer, bloody torture. I can't understand why it's happening."

The cat looked away, uninterested. *They must have their choosing,* said the taunting voice. *To be? Or not to be?*

11

"I CAN'T believe it," Veronica said. "That bruise is completely gone. And you look fine. The way Charles talked, you were at death's door."

Carol managed to smile, although the phrase "at death's door" resonated ominously. The gate would open one last time tonight. Would it lead to death, as Evan thought?

"Charles is a fussbudget," she said.

"Humph," Veronica said. "This is a waste of good chicken soup, then. Oh, well, I'm glad."

Veronica had dropped in unannounced, bearing a poinsettia, a thermos of chicken noodle soup and a big box of Christmas cookies. The soup and cookies were compliments of Alvin.

Carol loved her friend, but would rather she hadn't come. The last opening of the gate lay too heavily on her mind. Each time she looked at Veronica she wondered if this would be the last she would ever see of her.

"I'm so frisky that I sent Mrs. Tibbets home this morning," Carol lied. "I mean, I still felt under the weather yesterday, but it's amazing what a good night's sleep can do."

"Amazing, indeed," Veronica said. "But she's still going to look in on you, right? I mean everybody says head injuries are tricky."

"Absolutely," Carol said. "She'll check up on me every morning and every evening. And if I need help, well, she's right next door."

"Good," Veronica said. "And I owe you an apology."

"An apology? About what?"

"About Charles," Veronica said with a sardonic look. "You were right. He *was* being a meddlesome son of a gun. You know what he did? He broke your date with Mark Martinson."

"My date?" Carol said blankly. She had forgotten completely about the lawyer. And she'd promised to go to the theater with him tomorrow night.

Veronica nodded. "Didn't Charles even tell you about it?"

"No. What?"

"I ran into Mark in the library. He said he called here to find out if you liked Indian food. He'd heard about this great Indian restaurant. Well, he said, a man answered and told him you weren't going anywhere Friday night. He was very snotty, and Mark, frankly, was frosted about it."

Carol smiled wanly. Friday night seemed an eternity away, and Mark Martinson and Charles both seemed like people from another life, with no real connection to her.

"Well," Veronica said, warming to her subject, "I told Mark exactly what happened. That you had an accident, and that Charles just sort of moved in on you. That you had to call the police to get rid of him."

"Oh," Carol said numbly.

"I said I didn't think you'd be well enough to go out Friday night. But he said he'd call to see how you are and to change the date. You still want to go out with him, don't you?"

"Of course," Carol said, trying to sound enthusiastic. She knew that she'd failed miserably, so she added, "But he's not really a warm sort of person. You know what I mean?"

"Yeah," Veronica admitted. "I do. He is sort of a cold fish. I'm sorry. I guess I just noticed him because he was so pretty—for a white guy." She winked. "But Bill Keats doesn't seem cold. In fact, he seems pretty hot for you."

"Bill Keats?" Carol echoed. She had almost forgotten him, too, the other bachelor at Veronica's party, the man with hair as red as her own.

"Bill's been doing a lot of traveling for the company this week, troubleshooting. But Alvin says every time he phones in, he asks about you. He told Alvin he was going to ask you out as soon as his schedule's less insane. Alvin says he's *smitten*."

"Smitten? I hardly know him."

Veronica patted Carol's knee encouragingly. "Alvin hardly knew me before he made up his mind I was the one he wanted. You made a big impression on this guy. And let me tell you, I've got very good vibes about him."

Carol shrugged helplessly, not knowing what to say.

"Look," Veronica said earnestly, "I've got dependable vibes, and I trust them. Bill Keats is a good guy. Alvin says he's smart, very smart. He also says he's got a great reputation for integrity. He's got a sense of humor, he's got terrific shoulders and he's not bad-looking. You and he even have the same color hair. You'd have cute little carrot-topped kids."

Carol swallowed with difficulty. "It's a little early to be talking about kids."

"Maybe. Maybe not. I'm just telling you I have good feelings about this guy. You know, I think you could be happy with him. Really. He's a nice, down-to-earth guy, and I—I just have good feelings about you and him, that's all."

"He—" Carol faltered "—he seemed like a very nice man."

"Alvin says the guy is entirely genuine. Honey, if anybody knows you've got to kiss a lot of toads before you find the prince, it's me. And I sense prince material in Bill Keats."

Carol only shook her head as if she were amused. But she was not amused; she was suddenly frightened.

What if all that Veronica said was true? What if this was why Evan had warned her to come back to this reality and stay? Bill Keats seemed like a good man, a worthy man. Perhaps she could be content with him. There could be children, a family...

"I've got to go," Veronica said, rising. "We're having Alvin's niece over tonight. We're having company every night this week—why's the Christmas season so crazy? I can't wait to have Alvin to myself for a change, the old snuggle-bear."

Carol rose, too. She felt guilty and ungrateful. After all, last weekend, Alvin and Veronica had given up a night just for her to introduce her to Mark Martinson and Bill Keats. "Give him an extra snuggle for me," Carol said, her throat tight.

She walked Veronica to the door. Impulsively she hugged her friend and held her tightly. "Thanks," she said. "Nobody could ever have been a better friend to me than you."

Veronica returned the hug warmly, then waved her away. "Don't get so emotional. I'm not going anywhere. I'll call you tomorrow. I'm glad to see you looking so good. By the time Bill gets back in town you'll be ready to dance all night."

"Sure," said Carol. "And then some." When she closed the door after Veronica, she went to the window and watched Veronica cross the snowy lawn and go to her silver-colored car. A lump formed in Carol's throat.

Veronica was so loyal and giving, so warm and full of life. Could Carol really leave her behind, and dear, generous Alvin, too? And if she did, what would they think?

Veronica's car pulled out of the driveway, rolled down the slushy street and disappeared around the corner. Carol looked after her, although the street was now deserted and lifeless.

Lifeless.

What would people think, Carol wondered, if she simply disappeared? Her friends, her aunt, her colleagues? Who would teach her classes, counsel her students? What would happen to her belongings? There was the house, her car, her meager furniture, a bank account . . .

If she walked into the light and never came back, what should she do beforehand? Write a note of explanation? Everyone would think she was mad, of course.

She didn't have a will. If she wrote one now and left it, everyone would think she had gone somewhere and committed suicide. But that wasn't what she was contemplating—or was it?

The door buzzer made its rude noise, and she jumped, startled. She was expecting no one. Who could it be? Veronica returning, because she had forgotten something? Charles? She prayed it wasn't Charles.

But when she looked out the window, she saw no car, familiar or strange, in her driveway. A man she'd never seen before stood on her porch. He was a wizened little man in a worn jacket, and his wrinkled face was red with cold.

She swung open the door. He was elderly, slight and as short as she was. He wore no hat, and the winter wind had ruffled his thin gray hair.

His old-fashioned wire-rimmed glasses were taped at the nose piece, and one lens was chipped. He wore no gloves, so his hands were as red and roughened with cold as his face. He carried a small stack of flimsy pamphlets, and he looked flimsy himself, too frail to face the harsh December cold.

"Hello?" she said dubiously.

He smiled at her. "Good afternoon, sister," he said in a creaky little voice. "It's a bitter old day, isn't it?"

She nodded, puzzled.

"And it seems like a bitter old world sometimes, doesn't it? War and famine, famine and war. Violence everywhere. Sorrow and suffering, suffering and sorrow. Do you ever wonder what it all means?"

He stared at her with such cheerful earnestness that she was struck silent for a moment. Some sort of crusader, appearing on her doorstep, today of all days?

A familiar, aloof voice suddenly pierced her consciousness. *How now! What news?*

She turned and was surprised to see the cat, who usually fled when the door buzzer sounded. He stood in the shadows at the far end of the hall, staring at her. He switched his tail, as if in challenge. *Who's there, in the name of Beelzebub? Who's there in the devil's other name?*

He turned his back and stalked off into the dimness of the unlit kitchen. She faced the little old man again, her heart beating fast. She had the irrational instinct that he was there for a purpose, and that the cat knew it.

"Yes?" she said, studying the man more intently. He was so withered but genial that he reminded her of an elderly cricket who had somehow survived into midwinter, still able to chirp.

"Sister," he said, "all this hubbub and trouble is because we're in the last days. The end is nigh. But there's time to save yourself, sister. Oh, yes, there's just enough time."

She felt giddy, almost faint. Had They sent this inno-cent-seeming man? Or had he appeared, as if by magic, to fight Them? Or was it all simply bizarre coincidence?

"You look wary, sister," he said, hunching his shoulders against the cold. "Don't be. I represent no church, no organized religion at all. I'm a thinker and philosopher, come to share my message."

He jigged feebly as if trying to dance life back into his feet. He glanced down at the pamphlets in his thin hand. "I write and publish this message myself. It can change your life, sister. It can *save* your life."

Is that why you're here? she thought. *You've come to save my life? You're such a small, old, worn-out soldier to fight for my soul.*

"Only fifty cents, sister," he said in his merry, piping voice. "A small price to pay. Only fifty pennies. And a few minutes of your day. To talk about important things."

"To talk about important things," she echoed numbly. "You mean you've come to me on a mission."

Behind his mended glasses, his faded eyes shone brightly. "A mission? Exactly, sister. I've come to you on a special mission."

She appraised him for a long moment. He looked harmless, but since the cat had come, nothing was what it seemed. But the man's clothing told her he was poor, and the winter seemed to pierce his fleshless body.

"Would you like to come in and get warm?" she asked. "I—I could make you a cup of cocoa, perhaps?"

His wrinkled face lit. "Bless you, little sister. It's a hard day on my thin old blood."

She never let strangers into her house, but today she felt an odd recklessness. How, after all, could this man harm her? She was on the brink of such unknowns that ordinary dangers seemed puny, laughable.

She led him into the kitchen, sat him down at her table and began making a cup of instant cocoa.

"A big house," he said, looking about. "A fine, big house. But nearly empty? You're moving on somewhere?"

"Maybe," she said, sensing the irony. The cat was nowhere to be seen. She thought again of him running through the blue, glowing space, the hummingbird in his mouth. The hummingbird that was from Africa. The hummingbird that was dead, as if in warning.

She turned to face the little man, who was rubbing his reddened hands together. "Just what message did you come to bring me?" she asked, lifting her chin.

He took off his glasses, which had fogged from the change in temperature. He rubbed them on the sleeve of his faded jacket. He had a slight squint to one eye, and without his glasses, it gave him a look that was either wise or sly; she couldn't decide.

"My message?" he asked, then tapped the stack of pamphlets he'd set on the table. "It's right here. It's very simple. Do you know why people are unhappy?"

She shook her head. "For any number of reasons. For thousands of reasons."

"No," he said, putting on his glasses again. "People are unhappy for *one* reason. Desire. They always want what they haven't got. They should be satisfied with what they have."

The words shook her more than she let him see. "That's not much comfort to the hungry or homeless," she said.

"Ah!" he cried in triumph, raising his forefinger. "But if the rich didn't desire their wealth so much and lay up treasures for themselves, there would be no hungry. There would be no homeless."

"In a perfect world," she said, feeling hollow. "It can't happen in this one."

"No," he said emphatically. "It's because of the demons."

The teakettle had started to whistle. Hastily she took it from the burner and filled a mug. "Demons?" she said, trying to sound casual. She stirred the powdered cocoa mix into the cup. "What about them?"

"Everyone now," he said, chafing his hands again, "talks about angels, angels, angels. Angels are popular right now. Angels are a fad. Don't get me wrong. I'm not criticizing angels. No, no, no."

She set the mug before him, but remained standing. She leaned against the counter, crossing her arms. "You believe in angels?"

He took the mug gratefully, but didn't drink yet. He seemed content simply to clasp it with both hands, feeling its warmth.

"I certainly believe in angels. They protect us. But they don't walk around in wings and halos and bright robes. Oh, no, no, no."

Her pulses drummed so hard that she could hear the thudding of blood in her ears. She swallowed, but with difficulty, because her mouth was so dry.

"What form," she asked carefully, "might an angel take?"

"Ah," he said sagely, "that's the tricky part. They test us, you see. They come in *unexpected* forms."

She licked her lips, crossed her arms more tightly. "What happens if one comes to help you, and you don't recognize him—or her—or it?"

"Well, that's the peril, of course," he said. "Then you're skunked, so to speak." He raised the mug and sipped greedily at the cocoa.

"Skunked," she repeated sardonically.

"Skunked," he said. "So you've got to be alert. Or you could be sadly misled."

Her pulses drummed more fearfully. "Misled?"

"Yes," he said, narrowing his squinting eye at her. "Because while people stand around, staring at the sky, waiting for angels in white dresses to come down, the demons walk around, as big as you please. And they get away with murder sometimes. Yes, indeed. They get away with *murder*."

She squared her jaw, regarded him more somberly. "And just what form do demons take?" she asked, trying to keep her voice steady.

He took a long drink of the cocoa. It left a faint brown mustache on his withered upper lip. He narrowed his eye again.

"Now, your demons," he said, nodding, "they can take any form they like. But their favorite form—are you listening carefully, sister?—their favorite form is something you desire. Oh, yes. They disguise themselves as something you desire. It all fits together, you see."

It all fits together, she thought bitterly. *And none of it fits together*.

"And your demon," he continued, "isn't a physical being like you. He's all energy, evil energy. But he can use that energy to create the illusion of a body—just like yours or mine."

"It would seem absolutely real," she repeated, unable to keep a quaver out of her voice. "But it wouldn't be."

"Oh, as real as anything you can think of," he said. "You could see him, hear him, touch him. You could even smell him, and he'd seem like perfume to you. If you put out your tongue, you could taste him. He'd taste as sweet as pie."

Her heartbeat had become shallow and fast. It rattled her breastbone and threatened to choke her breath. "Why do you keep saying, 'he'?" she asked.

He ignored the question. He took out a dirty handkerchief and blew his nose, then dabbed at his nostrils. "Now, your demon, he'll tend to come to you in the most desirable form possible. That's your major death-dealing demon. He fools your mind, he takes your heart, he steals your soul, he drags you down to darkness and to death."

"Why do you keep saying, 'he'?" she demanded tightly.

Once more he let the question pass by. "Now, your minor demon," he went on, "he might disguise himself as anyone or anything. A cat, a rat, a bat, a fancy or a dream. A lust, a longing, a yearning or a burning. But plain or fancy, he'll try to lead you to a bad desire."

She stared at him as levelly as she could. "Why did you say 'cat'?" she asked.

He drained his cocoa, then wiped his palm across his lips. He stared longingly into his empty cup, as if wishing it were full again. "I was inspired to say 'cat,' I suppose. What's it matter if I say 'cat' or don't say 'cat'?"

"It doesn't matter," she said, but again she felt the unnerving certainty that he'd been sent. But why? To warn her or misguide her?

"That was mighty tasty, sister. Mighty. It almost warmed my cold old bones. It pretty near unthawed me."

She knew he was asking for another mug, but he frightened her. If he was right, she'd been fooled all along. If she went into the light, it was really darkness she would meet. She might think she was choosing love, but betrayal and loss and death were what she would reap.

She had always been a rational, objective, scientific person—until the cat had come. She had never believed in spirits, either good or evil. Now she no longer knew what was real or unreal, what to trust, what to doubt.

"Where does God fit into all this?" she asked him.

"That?" he said, still staring into the mug. "Oh, I don't bring that into it. It tends to divide people, talk like that. Set them apart. I aim to bring them together."

"You're nonsectarian?"

"That's the word," he said, and grinned up at her. "I'm nonsectarian." His smile made his wrinkles deepen; they seemed carved into his weathered face, a thousand of them.

"So desires are demons in disguise. And they'll always lie to you."

"Oh, not always," he said, cocking his head conspiratorially. "They're too smart for that. There's an old saying, something like 'Sometimes the dark powers tell us the truth. The little truths are baits, so we swallow the big lie.'"

She put her hand to her forehead. Tension made it ache. "I'm sorry," she said. "Maybe you'd better go now. I have things to do."

"Places to go?" he suggested brightly.

"Perhaps," she said. Perhaps. Oh, God, what was she going to do? What was she supposed to do?

"People to meet?"

She nodded unhappily. "Yes. Maybe . . . someone."

"Be careful," he warned. "Travel can be dangerous. And folks aren't always what they seem."

She opened her eyes and met his gaze, almost coldly. "I'm aware of that."

"Can I leave you one of my pamphlets?" he asked, patting the stack fondly. "It contains important advice. Things you need to know." Then he added, "That everybody needs to know, of course."

The little man, as frail and smiling as he was, had made her almost unbearably nervous. "Yes, yes," she said. "Leave one on the table. Fifty cents, you say? I'll pay you on the way out."

He rose as if reluctant to leave the house, but he beamed at her. "You're a kind lady, a good lady," he said. "I wish you a long, happy and virtuous life."

She fought against closing her eyes again. "A long, happy and virtuous life," she echoed. The words made her lips go stiff.

She picked up her purse from the living room couch, dropped two quarters into his outstretched hand, which was rather dirty. "Thank you," she said, opening the door for him. "And you really should get a hat and some gloves. It's biting cold outside."

"Good, kind lady," he repeated, smiling benevolently. "I'll see you again. I'll stop this way another time. We'll talk again."

"Yes, certainly," she said uneasily. He went out the door slowly, turning up his collar against the wind, which had risen.

She closed the door after him, grateful he was gone, and watched him trudge down the walk, his head ducked against the cold, the winter wind blowing his thin hair. In spite of his age and frailness, his step was almost spritely. He passed six other houses without stopping at them, then turned the corner and disappeared.

She stared after him, apprehensive again. Why had he called at no other house on this block except hers? He couldn't have visited the one house on the other side of hers; that was Rose's, and she was in Florida.

Again she had the odd, shuddery feeling that he had been sent to warn her against going to Shadowland. If the cat was always cryptic, the old man had made himself painfully clear: demons existed. They could assume any form, even the most desirable, in order to tempt one into ruin and death.

The thought that it was not Evan in Shadowland, but only some illusion spawned by evil frightened and repelled her. Yet she still had trouble believing in demons of any sort. And if they existed, why go to such trouble just for her?

Perhaps the old man's strange visit had been only a quirky coincidence. Perhaps he was a mere eccentric, full of peculiar notions. Yet his words haunted her.

Angels came in unexpected forms, he'd said, and not to recognize one was perilous. Could an angel appear on her doorstep as a wizened and threadbare old crank, with a dirty handkerchief and hands that were none too clean?

"I'm sinking into a morass of superstition," she whispered to herself. "I'm losing it." She went back into the kitchen to look at the pamphlet he had left lying on the table.

With distaste she picked up his empty mug, rinsed it off and washed her hands. Then she sat at the table and began to read the skimpy pamphlet. His name and address were stamped on the upper corner of the first page:

Francis Saintsbury
Economy Apartments #13b
Industrial Street
Verity, Illinois

He'd obviously typed the thing himself, and he was a poor typist and an indifferent speller. The pages had been printed on a copy machine that needed a cleaning and fresh ink. The little booklet consisted of only four pages stapled unevenly together.

"Francis Saintsbury, His Teachings of Truth!" read the masthead, "VolUme two, Issue FouR." The article on the first page was titled: "Further Thoughts on the Demons of Desire—Number Three—The Demon of Lust!"

"THe demon of lust is one oF you're more powerfull and potent demons and delites to take a pLeasing shape," Saintsbury had written.

"Sometimes these demons will even haunt you're dreams with images of lust so vivvid they asume the very semblance of reality. You would think you are in the Fair Arms of lOve, but in truTh you are in the embrace of a foRbiddden Tempter.

"These Dreams of so-Called physical delite take on the aspeck of actual Life and may be of sucH intensitty as to unhinge the very Mind itSelf, the Seat of reason. Such dreams may Haunt the Waking hOurs and make us dwell on what seems Love sweet Love, but what is in truth the road to darkest dispair and even worse."

"Oh!" Carol moaned softly, and leaned her elbow on the table, her forehead on her hand. Tears blurred her vision. It was too eerie, too bewildering; he might be writing for her alone. All her dreams of Evan had been sensual, exquisitely so, and astonishingly clear.

Words, words, words, said a cynical voice within her mind.

She whirled in her chair and saw that Shadow had stolen into the kitchen. He stood by his water dish, gazing at her with his unwavering pale green gaze.

Her jaw trembled in confusion and anger. "A very strange man was just here," she said. "He said you might be a—a minor demon. He said a demon could take a cat's form."

An honorable man, the voice said sarcastically, *wise and honorable.*

"Is he?" she challenged. "Is that the truth? Is he honest?"

He gave a languid blink. *Is he not honest?*

She struggled to control her emotions. "You only talk in riddles. He, at least, spoke straight out. He seemed more straightforward than you ever do."

Men should be what they seem, he said. Then he turned his back on her and daintily lapped water from his dish.

She resisted the desire to fling the pamphlet at him. She propped her hands on either side of her head in despair. She saw Saintsbury's title again: "Further Thoughts on the Demons of Desire," and looked away.

"He might be a demon himself," she said bitterly. "Or he might be an angel. Or he might be just a strange old man."

The cat strolled to the table and sat down next to her chair. *What he might be, he is not.*

"See?" she almost spat. "More riddles. If he's not devil, angel or man, what is he?"

The cat scratched his ear with his hind foot. He closed his eyes in concentration. *What you know, you know,* he said.

"I know nothing," she said in frustration. "Not what you are, not what he is. Not even what Evan is, real or—or something else."

The cat stopped scratching. *Be not afraid,* the voice said smugly. *I and my fellows are ministers of fate.*

"Ministers of fate," she mocked. "More like imps of the perverse. And what about that hummingbird? How did you get it? Where did you get it?"

He cocked his head. The voice became almost singsong.

Through flood, through fire,
I do wander everywhere.

She glared at him, her eyes bright with unshed tears of angry dismay. "And what was it supposed to mean? That you could lead us to a place like Tanzania? Or someplace where we'd be dead as the bird?"

Our doubts are traitors, the voice crooned. *And make us lose the good we oft might win.*

He rose and paced soundlessly toward the hall.

"Don't go yet," she ordered. "I want answers from you, dammit."

His ears pricked more sharply at her swearword. He turned and looked coolly over his shoulder. *Seek to know no more.*

"I said I want answers!"

The rest is silence, he said with finality. He turned his back on her again and walked away.

She started to rise and follow him, to shake a straight reply from him if she had to, but just then, her door buzzer made its loud, grating sound.

Her heart leaped, and she felt simultaneously burning and chilled at once. Who now? she thought.

She was expecting no one. She had wanted no one to come. Who was this third uninvited caller?

12

JERRY BRATLING, his face nearly hidden by the fur-edged hood of his parka, stood at the door. His hands were jammed deeply into his pockets.

"Hi, kiddo," he said, his breath pluming up like silvery smoke. "Carmen said if I didn't check on you on the way home, she'd divorce me. Am I interrupting anything?"

Only a conversation I was having with the cat, she thought ironically. *But he seemed to think it was over anyway.*

"Not at all," she said. "Won't you come in, have a cup of coffee?"

She tried to sound pleased that he was there. In truth, she was leery, afraid she would blurt out something odd that would set off his suspicions.

Yet he might be the very person she needed—she didn't know. She could no longer think clearly; she was too mystified, too torn and bewildered.

"Come in, yes," he said with a sideways smile. "Coffee, no. I'll just stay a few minutes."

She led him inside and gestured toward the couch. He pushed back his parka hood, stripped off his gloves, unzipped the parka and sat. She seated herself across from him in the room's lone armchair.

He polished the fog from his glasses and put them back on, peering at her. "You look chipper," he said. "About a hundred percent better than yesterday. How are you feeling?"

"Chipper," she said, forcing a smile. "Two hundred percent better. No more headache, vision's perfect, no drowsiness. Good as new. How's Carmen?"

"Fine. Great with child and just as great in attitude. Push your bangs back. How's the bruise?"

Reluctantly, she brushed her curly bangs back to reveal her temple and hairline. Jerry's usual cool expression turned to one of surprise.

"Good grief," he said. "I can't even see it. That's amazing. Can I look closer?"

She shrugged. "Sure. But it's no big deal. I heal fast, that's all. Always have."

He rose and bent over her. He touched her temple with clinical detachment. "Does it feel tender here?"

"Not a bit. Like I say, I heal fast."

Jerry shook his head. "I never saw anybody heal *that* fast. Not a trace of it left. Amazing." He shook his head and returned to the couch.

Carol let her bangs fall back into place. "So you see," she said, "I'm fine. No need to worry about me."

He nodded but studied her intently. "What about dreams, fancies, things like that? Anything strange been cropping up there?"

She tensed. If she told the truth, he'd want her to check into a hospital immediately. If she lied, that meant she'd decided to go to Shadowland again, to step back into the unknown, despite all the warnings.

She decided half-truths were her safest course. "I've had some strange dreams," she said. "I dreamed that Evan was alive, but not here. In another place."

"Another place?" Jerry drew one bushy brow down in a frown. "Where?"

She made a helpless gesture. "Just this strange place. I can't describe it. A sort of twilight zone."

She was silent a moment, pondering how much else she should say. "In this—this dream," she said carefully, "it was as if I could join him. But I couldn't come back to this world. He told me to stay here."

"And?" Jerry prodded gently. "Anything else?"

She composed herself, spoke slowly and thoughtfully. "And there were other warnings. That I shouldn't join him again. Or that I should be careful."

"Other warnings?" Jerry echoed. "From whom?"

"Oh, it's vague. You know how dreams are. An old man, I think. I can't remember who else."

"The cat?" Jerry suggested, looking calmly unconcerned. "Felix Sternberger said the cat figured in your dreams a lot."

The cat figured in her reality a lot, far too much, perhaps, but she didn't wish to tell that to Jerry. "Maybe he did," she lied. "I can't remember."

"Hmm," he said noncommittally. "Can you recall the actual warnings?"

"Let me see," she hedged. "That's vague, too. Mostly just that if I tried to go to Evan, I'd be dealing with unknown forces. Maybe dangerous forces."

"Hmm." His gaze fell to her wrist, resting on the silver ID bracelet she still wore.

"So," she said with simulated cheeriness, "what does that mean? That my brains banged a little too hard when I fell? I mean, it was only one more dream."

He sighed. "I thought you weren't going to wear that bracelet anymore."

She smiled as if she were unconcerned. "Oh, I'll take it off. I forget I have it on, actually."

He nodded silently, then gazed into her eyes, his expression gentle and a little sad. "It's really been hard for you to let go, hasn't it, Carol?"

She forced a smile. "I suppose. But the dream, Jerry. What's it mean? Do you believe in supernatural forces?"

He gave a dubious snort. "Absolutely not. If I did, I'd give up psychiatry and take up witch doctoring. Why? Are you getting interested in the supernatural?"

"Or course not," she said. "That's why I asked you what the dream meant."

"The dream," he said, rubbing his chin thoughtfully. "Actually, I think it might be a good one. You found Evan, but not in this world. He told you to go back. So did an old man. An old man is often a symbol of our inner wisdom."

Carol swallowed uncomfortably. "He is?"

Jerry nodded. "He is. He signifies what we must learn to be whole. And the message is clear. To be whole, you must stop trying to find Evan. It's unwholesome and dangerous for you."

"Oh" was all she could say.

"Our dreams often send us signals. Your deep inner self knows that you must put Evan behind and go on. With a life here and not in some 'Twilight Zone.'"

"Oh," she said again.

"Keep track of these dreams," he urged. "I think your unconscious mind is urging you to heal, at long last. You keep taking note of the dreams. We'll talk about them."

"Certainly," she said, then added, "I'll . . . keep a notebook."

"Excellent." He smiled. "Just the way I remember you in grad school. Practical and efficient. Anything else you'd like to talk about?"

She paused. She should ask him a hundred questions. A thousand. "No," she said at last. "I guess not."

"Then I'd better get home to Carmen," he said, rising and zipping up his parka. "And we'll talk in more depth tomorrow."

"Tomorrow?" she asked, caught off guard. She'd forgotten she had an appointment to see him tomorrow. "Oh, of course," she said. "Yes, tomorrow afternoon."

He pulled on his gloves. "And I know you seem to have made a speedy recovery. But don't drive. Take a cab or have somebody bring you. A head injury is tricky, Carol. You can be feeling fine, then—bam—it sneaks back up on you. You don't even know what hit you."

She made her tone light, almost bantering. "You mean I could suddenly start seeing things and have to be taken off to the cracker factory?"

He smiled ruefully. "It's happened, but that's not what I'm worried about. Just be careful for the next few weeks. If the headache returns, or the drowsiness, any vision problems, let me know at once."

"I will," she promised.

"If you sense anything out of the ordinary, *anything*," he said, "contact me. Anytime, night or day. It doesn't matter. You're more than a friend to Carmen and me. We all went through so much back then, it's almost like you're family."

"Why, thank you," she said, touched, but saddened, as well, by her own untruthfulness.

"So, is the old boyfriend keeping his distance?" he asked as they walked to the door.

"Yes. He is."

"Good," Jerry said. "But try to find a new one, somebody not quite so obsessive-compulsive."

"I will," she vowed, feeling falser and more treacherous by the second.

"And your neighbor lady?" he asked, pulling up the hood of his parka. "I don't see her. Is she still staying with you?"

"No," Carol said brightly. "I felt so great I sent her home. But she's going to look in on me twice a day."

He nodded. "Good. I hope you're not going back to work for a while."

"Not until Monday," she said. "I'll be so rested that I'm restless. So relaxed it'll make me nervous."

He smiled fondly. "Moderation in all things. Take care, kiddo. I'll see you tomorrow."

"Yes," she said, wondering if she would or not.

When he left, she closed the door, then wandered back to the kitchen. Dear, sweet, kindly, concerned Jerry, she thought, hating herself for hiding things from him.

Yet she couldn't believe she was insane and that Shadowland was only an illusion. Evan had been too real in her arms. The cat did speak directly to her mind; she was certain. But Jerry would only think she was unbalanced.

She smiled bitterly. Didn't most psychopaths insist they were sane? Didn't nearly all of them think their delusions were hard facts? Was she simply a classic case of someone losing her grip on reality?

She sat down moodily at the table again. She stared at Francis Saintsbury's crude pamphlet. She opened it.

"How to Overcome the Demons of Lust," read a subheading. She stared at the advice numbly.

To Vanquish the demons of lustful desire
practice the Following:

1. Exercise the Body and dIscipline it.
2. Do not eat the Flesh of animals because they re-
produce through copulation and you are what you
eat.
3. Teach you're own flesh Humility. Let it be cold in
winter and Sweat in summer. Take cold baths, Never
warm . . .

The list went on, but she pushed it away from her. Jerry
said that an old man in a dream symbolized inner wisdom. But this old man had been no dream.

At least, he had seemed real. But had he come to give
her words of wisdom? Or had everything he'd said been
a meaningless muddle?

Evan had believed he and she were being tested, tempted
somehow. Was the old man part of the test? And if he was,
which was right? To reject what he'd told her or to accept
it?

Her mind spun helplessly, and she leaned her elbows on
the table, put her face in her hands. Then she heard the
muted jingle of a bell.

She looked up. Shadow had made his way into the
kitchen and sat in the doorway, staring at her. *A sad tale's
boot for winter*, the taunting voice said. *I have one of
sprites and goblins.*

"Sprites and goblins? I'll bet you do," she said contemptuously. "Back to mock me? Haven't you something
nasty to say about my friend? The one who just left?"

Once again the voice turned sarcastically singsong:

He that is a friend indeed,
He will help thee in thy need.

She narrowed her eyes at him. "Then he is my friend. He always has been. What does that make you?"

He switched his tail with an almost insolent slowness. He half closed his eyes. *We must not be foes.* He yawned.

"You spoke of sprites and goblins. Which are you? Goblin? Sprite?"

He stood and padded to the window. He leaped to the sill and stared out at the falling night. *I am not what I am.*

Suddenly he pricked his black ears higher and turned back toward the room. He tilted his head, first this way, then that, as if he could hear things inaudible to her. He somehow looked slyer than he usually did.

Her skin prickled with apprehension. "What is it?" she asked. "What do you hear?"

His left ear twitched slightly, then his right. He met her gaze. *The inaudible and noiseless foot of time,* he said in his superior way.

For a moment, she, too, listened. The house was as silent as a grave, but she thought that she could also hear the tread of time, and that it echoed heavily in the still air.

"I can almost hear it," she whispered, more to herself than the cat. She stared up at the shadowy corners of the ceiling. "Will it be soon? Now that it's dark? When the gate opens again?"

Soon enough, said the aloof voice. *Be patient.*

She almost laughed. "How can I be patient? I'm supposed to choose. But how can I choose? I think that I doubt everything, then something comes and makes me doubt still more."

The cat lifted one black shoulder as if in a shrug of dismissal. *There will be three come to tempt you today. Nay, lady, four, and I do not count myself.*

She sucked in her breath and tried to order her spinning thoughts. She had indeed had three visitors today, Veronica, the old man and Jerry Bratling.

She said, "You tempted me to go to Evan in the first place, to cross that threshold of light. The others tell me to build my life here. It's safe and certain here. But where you'd lead me—"

Is wondrous strange.

"Strange, yes? But false? Or insane? Or evil?"

What you know, you know.

"And you say a fourth person's coming? What for?" she demanded. "To confuse me even more?"

The phone rang. She started to tremble in apprehension. It rang again. Who was calling? Was this the fourth person the cat had predicted?

Shadow looked smug.

"Devil," she said between her teeth.

You charge me most unjustly. He looked still colder and more smug.

She stiffened her shoulders, turned her back on him and hurried to answer the phone. "Hello?"

A deep, friendly, easy voice answered her.

"Carol? This is Bill Keats. We met at Veronica's party."

"Oh," she said. "Yes. Of course." She didn't remember his voice as being that resonant, that appealing.

"I said I'd call," he told her. "I've been on the run so much, it's been hard. I'm in Boston. But I didn't want to wait any longer."

"It—it's nice to hear from you," she managed to say. "Veronica was just talking about you this morning."

She could see him in her mind's eye: tall, broad shouldered, a strongly built man. His face was homely-handsome, with strong, even features and lively blue eyes. He had fiery hair and far more freckles than even she had.

"I talked to Alvin this afternoon," Bill Keats said. "He said you'd had an accident. I hope it wasn't serious."

He sounded relaxed, but she found it hard to speak. "A fall down the stairs," she said. "I had a bad day or so, but I'm fine now. Good as new."

"Glad to hear it. You sound good. I didn't remember you had such a nice voice. I guess I was too busy listening to what you said, not how you said it."

"Oh," she responded lamely, "thank you."

"I've been thinking about you," he said. "I really would like to see you again. Alvin talked as if he thought the world of you. After I met you, I saw why."

"He—he spoke highly of you, too."

He laughed. "I'm just an average Joe. But you and I seemed to like some of the same things. I haven't seen the Museum of Natural History yet. I suppose you know it inside out."

She did, of course. She knew it by heart. It had been one of the first places she'd intended to take Evan when he came back to the States and to her.

"I know it, yes," she said, her throat constricted.

"I have to go to Connecticut, then New Hampshire, then New York. I'm staying an extra day in New York to be with my brother and his wife. They've got three little boys, like stair steps. All with hair as red as fire. Cutest little guys you ever saw."

She remembered Veronica's remark that she and Bill Keats would have darling red-haired children. She tried to swallow the knot rising in her throat. "It sounds wonderful," she said.

"I'm a sucker for kids," he said with a chuckle. "I like playing uncle. I want to enjoy them while I can. They grow up so fast."

"Yes," she said mechanically. "They do." She glanced around the big, empty room. Once she had imagined this house loud and lively with four children, two boys, two girls.

"I'll get back late Friday," he said. "If you'd show me the museum Saturday afternoon, I'd love to buy you supper that night. Alvin suggested this restaurant in Old Town. He says it's top-notch."

"If Alvin says so, it is."

"Does that mean yes?" he asked. "I thought after supper we might go to the Second City comedy review. I heard it's really a good season."

"I've . . . heard that, too," she said, trying to keep her voice from shaking.

"I guess it's presumptuous of me to ask you to spend so much time with me," he said. "But I really have been thinking of you, Carol. And I do want to know you better. When you walked into Veronica's living room and gave that shy little smile, I just . . . wanted to know you a whole lot better."

She could think of nothing to say. He'd been a warm, unpretentious man, charming in a folksy way. He was easy to talk to, easy to like, and he had an air of solid dependability.

"So," he said, "just tell me? Does that sound at all appealing to you? Would you say yes? I'd love it if you'd say yes."

She shut her eyes. She could imagine herself with him, comfortable and safe and friendly. She could imagine him, almost, as a husband, just as Veronica had suggested. She could even envision, dimly, a little red-haired child pulling at his trouser legs, looking up at him in affection, calling him "Daddy."

"Yes," she found herself saying. "It sounds like a—a wonderful sort of day."

"Great," he said with enthusiasm. "Now, for the next couple weeks, I've got all this stupid traveling. But then I get to stay put, settle down for a change. Am I glad."

He went on, talking about buying season tickets for the White Sox games, asking her what kind of movies and plays she liked, telling her he liked the same. He asked about her family, told her a bit more about his.

"Gee, I'm talking your ear off," he said. "But it's really been nice. I'll look forward to seeing you Saturday. I'll look forward to it a lot."

"Yes," she said, rather weakly. "Me, too."

"Could I pick you up at about one o'clock?"

"Th-that would be fine. Yes. One o'clock will be fine."

"Perfect," he said. "I'll see you then." ·

"Yes," she breathed. "I'll see you then."

She felt strangely empty when she hung up. She turned from the phone and saw the cat standing across the room, watching her. His tail switched languidly.

So? the voice in her mind hissed. *This is your choosing?*

"I don't know," she said miserably. "I don't know about anything anymore. What could be worse then this damned choosing?"

Choosing wrong, the voice replied without hesitation.

She jerked her chin up truculently. "You know what that old man—that Francis Saintsbury would say you're tempting me with?"

The cat blinked calmly. *Death and damnation.*

"Precisely," she retorted. "And Jerry Bratling would call you the illusion of a distraught mind."

But that's a fable.

"Is it? Veronica is my true friend. She told me to get on with my life, that Bill Keats is a good man, good for me. And she's Miss Common Sense."

The cat gave his tail another slow switch.

"Evan himself told me not to follow you again. He said to make a life without him. With someone like Bill Keats I could have—"

A dull, stale, tired bed, he said contemptuously. *Go. Go to the creating of a whole tribe of fops.*

The words stung so painfully that she turned from him. "At least it's not a bed alone," she said. "Or one in the earth. A grave. Bill Keats is a—a comfortable man."

Such men are dangerous.

She whirled to face him. "You say that. But you've also told me you're not completely truthful."

When truth kills truth, O devilish-holy fray.

She put her fingertips to her temples. "What am I supposed to believe?"

The steadiness of his green gaze was almost hypnotic. *Believe me, King of Shadows. I have looked on truth askance and strangely.*

"What happens to Evan if I don't go to him? He said that They—whoever They are—would send him to another place. What becomes of him? Where will he be?"

Fled from this vile world, with vilest worms to dwell.

Hot tears sprang to her eyes. "Dead? Just…dead? What happens if I go to him?"

The voice became silky, almost supplicating. *O, never say that I was false of heart.*

"False of heart?" she asked, her mouth twisting. "You may be false of everything. You might be the very essence of deceit, for all I know."

The cat turned away, looking bored. The voice in her mind sighed tiredly. It said, *They must have their choosing. They will have it, lady. Have it, they will.*

He stepped into the hall and melted into its shadows. She knew better than to try to follow him. She flung herself down on the couch and wept uncontrollably. At last, exhausted, she wept herself to sleep.

Her sleep for once was dreamless, as dark and empty as if it were a little piece of death.

SHE WAS AWAKENED by a soft thump near her feet, and something like velvet touched her bare flesh. Her eyes fluttered open. With a start, she saw that Shadow sat on the couch, his paw upon her ankle. When he seemed sure she was awake, he drew his paw away and shook it, as if in distaste.

"What is it?" she asked, her heart starting to beat harder. But she was afraid she knew. He was summoning her to face the light for the last time.

There's knocking at the gate: come, come, come, come.

Her heart drummed harder still. It was true; They had opened the gate into Shadowland again. His invitation played through her mind again, mocking her. *Come, come, come, come.*

She sat up straight and looked at him distrustfully. "It's time, isn't it?" she asked, although she knew the answer.

The iron tongue of midnight hath told twelve.

She found it hard to get her breath. She looked numbly at her watch. "Midnight," she whispered.

The cat drew back his head slightly, making him look haughtier than ever. He half closed his eyes. *'Tis now the very witching time of night.*

She was frightened, never before had she been so frightened. For a giddy second she thought of calling Jerry Bratling, of telling him everything.

The cat seemed to read her mind. *Our fears do make us traitors*, he admonished. He leaped from the couch and paced soundlessly into the hall.

She didn't hesitate. She rose and followed him. She could look at the light one last time; that did not mean she would enter it. Evan himself had told her not to come again. She could stay here, in earthbound reality, marry a man like Bill Keats, have a family, be happy . . .

She turned on the hall light. Shadow was already at the top of the stairs, where the dark began. He turned and gazed down at her, his eyes shining in the dimness.

Coldhearted toward me?

"Cold minded," she replied with bitterness. "I think you came to do me harm."

His very posture was scornful. *You are like the lunatic. He who sees more devils than vast hell can hold.*

He turned and vanished in the darkness of the upper hall. Slowly, her pulses thumping with anxiety, she climbed the steps. When she reached the top, she switched on the upstairs light.

She stood, staring down the hall. The cat was at the far end, before the door of the tower bedroom. He rubbed against its door sensuously, as if he loved it.

Come, come, come, come, the voice beckoned. Back and forth he rubbed the length of his body against the door. *Come, come, come, come.*

She took a long, shuddering breath. Squaring her shoulders, she made her way down the hall. She found herself before the door. Near her feet the cat rubbed against it still, back and forth, back and forth.

She thought, *I have to go see Jerry tomorrow. I have an appointment. I have to be back at school on Monday. I have two classes, office hours and a faculty meeting.*

Next Wednesday is my aunt's birthday, she thought. *I should drive to Elmhurst and see her. And take her present. I haven't even wrapped her present yet.*

On Saturday, she told herself, *I'm going to the Museum of Natural History with Bill Keats. I told him I would. And it will be that start of something between us. Veronica's right—I can feel it. I'm . . . attracted to him.*

Her heart knocked against her ribs. *But,* she thought, *I can look one last time before I get on with my life. I can look and say goodbye.*

She put her hand on the knob, turned it, pushed the heavy door open. She gasped and took a step backward, snatching her hand away from the knob. This time the room was full of light, top to bottom.

No, she amended, staring in horrified fascination. There was no longer top or bottom to the room, nor were there any walls. On the other side of the door was an infinity of blue light, still and silent.

This time, she thought, *They must have thrown the gate completely open. So she could enter for good and not return.* How long it would be open, she did not know, could not even guess.

Her face felt stiff, as if she were going to cry again. "I can't leave here," she told the cat. "I have friends here, people I—love." But none, she thought unhappily, whom she loved as much as she loved Evan.

The cat stared up, scorn in his eyes. *The best in their kind are but shadows.*

This time she could not doubt the truth of what he said. Compared with Evan, with his vitality and passion, all other people seemed like shadows, even herself.

But she shook her head. "Then they're the shadows I have to live with and love," she said grimly.

He used the teasing singsong tone she hated so much.
Some there be that shadows kiss;
Such but have a shadow's bliss.

That, too, she supposed was true. She would stay on this side, living a life that would never seem quite real to her after her time with Evan. Kissing another man would be like kissing a shadow. Any contentment she found would seem only the shadow of contentment.

But she must stay here. Evan himself had told her so. Her friends had counseled her in that vein, and Bill Keats was reaching out to her, showing she no longer had to be alone. The strange little man had come like a supernatural messenger to warn her to stay here, where she was.

"I wish," she said, her voice taut, "that you would tell me one true thing. Just one."

The cat had stopped his rubbing. He walked around her slowly, as if taking her measure. At last the low voice spoke in her mind again.

Love's not time's fool.

"What?" she asked, startled.

Love's not time's fool.

"But I don't understand—"

Before she could say more, the cat stepped forward. He disappeared into the blue light. The voice, ghostly, echoed once more in her mind. *Love's not time's fool.*

She stood, clenching and unclenching her fists, and fresh tears stung her eyes. She blinked them back, bit her lower lip. She could not follow this time.

To follow would be to fly in the face of all that was sane. She had no idea what lay in wait for her beyond the light— madness, death, damnation? No. She could not go.

But, she thought with a rush of recklessness, there was the faintest chance, surely almost impossible, that she could be with Evan again. There was that chance, no matter how small, how faint, how improbable. She might be reunited with him, if she was brave enough to go to him, if she loved him enough . . .

She closed her eyes, feeling dizzy and frightened. She remembered what They had told Evan. *Sometimes, if you love enough . . . Sometimes, if you love enough . . .*

Whoever They were, They had made no promises of a happy ending. And she knew They were capable of inflicting pain and probably worse. But the words haunted her, called to her.

Sometimes, if you love enough . . .

She opened her eyes. She smiled to herself a bit shakily. And she stepped into the light.

She was in Evan's strong arms, kissing him madly, hungrily, tearfully, happily.

"Carol," he said against her lips. "You shouldn't have come. We don't know—"

"I had to be with you," she said, and kissed him again.

Then, suddenly, she sensed change around them. The blue emptiness that surrounded them grew brighter, more intense. It began to vibrate strangely.

He held her tightly, and she clung to him. They both looked around fearfully. She saw the black cat, loping gracefully away from them through space, his feet touching nothing but light. Over his head flew a bird, its wings moving so rapidly they were a blur.

"The hummingbird," Evan said in wonder, drawing her more securely to him. "It's alive again—"

But then the light turned so bright it blazed into whiteness. Evan was still in her arms, and she in his, but she could no longer see him; she was blinded by light. And she had a giddy sensation that they were falling, falling more and more quickly, and although she was frightened, it was all happening too fast for her to scream and then . . .

SHE AND EVAN WERE camping in Tanzania, high on the crest of the volcano. The volcano had been inactive for centuries, and scientists said it would never erupt again. Yet Carol thought it wrong to call the volcano dead, for it was host to so much life.

The rich volcanic earth sprouted lush grasses, a wealth of wildflowers and exotic trees. Below, the rolling savanna teemed with wildlife, and a herd of elephants grazed, bathed in the crooked river and tended their young.

When night fell, the sky was velvety blue and spangled with uncountable stars. Evan pointed out the constellations they wouldn't be able to see when they were back home in North America. The half-moon hung low, huge and pocked and silvery blue.

They sat looking up at the sky, his arm around her, her head on his shoulder. "Know what I like about camping?" he asked in a lazy voice.

"What?" she said, just as lazily.

"Nothing to do after the sun goes down. Except stare at the sky awhile, then go to bed."

"Bed?" she asked innocently.

"Bed," he said with conviction. He gazed up at the star-strewn sky again. He shook his head. "It's so untouched here. I feel like we're in Eden."

"Yes," she said, and nuzzled the strong, warm column of his neck.

He turned to her, putting his hands on her shoulders. "Except," he drawled, "Eve didn't have all these pesky clothes."

"Oh?" she said a bit breathlessly. "Well, you're a man of action. Do something about it."

His hands moved to the top button of her camp shirt. "I never," he said, "turn down a challenge."

He made love to her so slowly, so thoroughly, so beautifully, that he made her feel like a goddess in the embrace of a handsome and powerful god. She had never imagined being this happy. She had not known it was possible.

At dawn they awoke to find the volcano's peak lost in a sea of white clouds. Nearby there was the drowsy twitter of birds. Far below them, the elephants trumpeted, welcoming the dawn.

But up above, at the crater's grassy edge, the dawn was only that unreal, soft whiteness. They might have been lying in heaven, so pure was the white, so coolly pleasant was its still air.

"What is it?" she breathed against Evan's neck, holding him more tightly. "Fog?"

"Clouds, love," he said, his lips close to her ear. "We're in the clouds."

She laughed softly, delighted by the thought. If she closed her eyes, all she saw was darkness. If she opened them, all she saw was the shifting, silvery white. And from the river came the haunting cry of the elephants calling to one another.

"It's like magic," she said. "It's like waking to the first morning of the world."

"It is," he murmured.

He held her in silence for a long moment, his naked body warm against hers.

Then he kissed her ear and said, "Last night we played around so much that I went off too fast. How about if I try to do it very, very slo-owly. Or are you worn out?"

It was the morning of the world, and she loved him so extravagantly that she felt she could never weary of it. "Oh, Evan," she said, nestling closer to him, "maybe this really *is* heaven." Then she laughed softly, because without meaning to, she'd made a rhyme: Evan, heaven.

"Maybe it is," he answered, and unzipped the sleeping bag. They made love on top of it again, their only covering the clouds.

IT WAS TO BE their last good memory of Africa. By the time they'd gotten back to Ibadan, Evan had fallen mysteriously sick. At last the doctors diagnosed the illness as a particularly nasty strain of noninfectious hepatitis.

He was sent back to the States to recuperate, and Carol, unable to have him sick and so far away, got special permission to join him. Within a few months, he had recovered, but they would both always regret having to leave Africa so early.

They found a wonderful old ramshackle house in the suburbs. It was Victorian, with a double staircase and a strange octagonal tower that was a bedroom. The room had a huge antique bed bolted down to a dais in its center.

Their first child was conceived on that bed in that octagonal bedroom. So were their three other children. Carol sometimes remarked that she felt as if the house were magical. Evan laughed at her fancy, but didn't contradict her.

Other people often commented on how devoted the two of them were, how they still seemed as deeply in love as newlyweds. Their big house was full of laughter and life. The children had dogs, fish, birds, gerbils, even a tame ferret.

And Carol had a black cat. For some reason she couldn't understand, she had come back from Africa suddenly very partial to black cats. When she got him, she didn't know what to name him.

"How about Shadow?" Evan suggested. He said he didn't know why he'd thought of that particular name, except the cat sometimes seemed to move as quietly as a Shadow.

"Good enough," Carol said, picking up the purring cat. Evan put his arms around her from behind and kissed her on the ear. "I love you," he said quietly.

She kissed the edge of his jaw. "I love you, too," she said. The cat purred and purred.

HARLEQUIN®
Temptation®

Secret Fantasies

Do you have a secret fantasy?

Small-town waitress Ellen Montrose does. At night she dreams of the Whitfield mansion, of dancing in the ballroom with a handsome sexy stranger. But fantasy and reality start to mysteriously collide when Ellen meets the man of her dreams—in the flesh—at the diner. Enjoy #538 THE MAN FROM SHADOW VALLEY by Regan Forest, available in May 1995.

Everybody has a secret fantasy. And you'll find them all in Temptation's exciting new yearlong miniseries—Secret Fantasies. Beginning January 1995, one book each month focuses on the hero or heroine's innermost romantic desires....

SF-5

MILLION DOLLAR SWEEPSTAKES (III)

MOVE OVER, MELROSE PLACE!

Apartment for rent
One bedroom
Bachelor Arms
555-1234

Come live and love in L.A. with the tenants of Bachelor Arms. Enjoy a year's worth of wonderful love stories and meet colorful neighbors you'll bump into again and again.

When Blythe Fielding planned her wedding and asked her two best friends, Caitlin and Lily, to be bridesmaids, none of them knew a new romance was around the corner for each of them—not even the bride! These entertaining, dramatic stories of friendship, mystery and love by JoAnn Ross continue the exploits of the residents of Bachelor Arms and answer one very important question: Will Blythe ever get to walk down the aisle? Find out in:

NEVER A BRIDE (May 1995) #537

FOR RICHER OR POORER (June 1995) #541

THREE GROOMS AND A WEDDING (July 1995) #545

Soon to move into Bachelor Arms are the heroes and heroines in books by always popular Candace Schuler and Judith Arnold. A new book every month!

Don't miss the goings-on at Bachelor Arms.

BA4

HARLEQUIN®
Temptation

THREE GROOMS:
Case, Carter and Mike

TWO WORDS:
"We Don't!"

ONE MINISERIES:

GROOMS ON THE RUN

Starting in May 1995, Harlequin Temptation
brings you an exciting miniseries called

GROOMS ON THE RUN

Each book (and there'll be one a month for three
months!) features a sexy hero who's ready to say,
"I do!" but ends up saying, "I don't!"

Watch for these special Temptations:

In May, **I WON'T!** by Gina Wilkins #539
In June, **JILT TRIP** by Heather MacAllister #543
In July, **NOT THIS GUY!** by Glenda Sanders #547

Available wherever Harlequin books are sold.

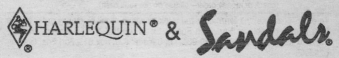

HARLEQUIN®

Don't miss these Harlequin favorites by some of our most
distinguished authors!
And now, you can receive a discount by ordering two or more titles!

HT #25607	PLAIN JANE'S MAN by Kristine Rolofson	$2.99 U.S./$3.50 CAN.	☐
HT #25616	THE BOUNTY HUNTER by Vicki Lewis Thompson	$2.99 U.S./$3.50 CAN.	☐
HP #11674	THE CRUELLEST LIE by Susan Napier	$2.99 U.S./$3.50 CAN.	☐
HP #11699	ISLAND ENCHANTMENT by Robyn Donald	$2.99 U.S./$3.50 CAN.	☐
HR #03268	THE BAD PENNY by Susan Fox	$2.99	☐
HR #03303	BABY MAKES THREE by Emma Goldrick	$2.99	☐
HS #70570	REUNITED by Evelyn A. Crowe	$3.50	☐
HS #70611	ALESSANDRA & THE ARCHANGEL by Judith Arnold	$3.50 U.S./$3.99 CAN.	☐
HI #22291	CRIMSON NIGHTMARE by Patricia Rosemoor	$2.99 U.S./$3.50 CAN.	☐
HAR #16549	THE WEDDING GAMBLE by Muriel Jensen	$3.50 U.S./$3.99 CAN.	☐
HAR #16558	QUINN'S WAY by Rebecca Flanders	$3.50 U.S./$3.99 CAN.	☐
HH #28802	COUNTERFEIT LAIRD by Erin Yorke	$3.99	☐
HH #28824	A WARRIOR'S WAY by Margaret Moore	$3.99 U.S./$4.50 CAN.	☐

(limited quantities available on certain titles)

	AMOUNT	$
DEDUCT:	**10% DISCOUNT FOR 2+ BOOKS**	$
ADD:	**POSTAGE & HANDLING**	$
	($1.00 for one book, 50¢ for each additional)	
	APPLICABLE TAXES*	$_____
	TOTAL PAYABLE	$_____
	(check or money order—please do not send cash)	

To order, complete this form and send it, along with a check or money order for the
total above, payable to Harlequin Books, to: **In the U.S.:** 3010 Walden Avenue,
P.O. Box 9047, Buffalo, NY 14269-9047; **In Canada:** P.O. Box 613, Fort Erie, Ontario,
L2A 5X3.

Name: _____

Address: _____ City: _____

State/Prov.: _____ Zip/Postal Code: _____

*New York residents remit applicable sales taxes.
 Canadian residents remit applicable GST and provincial taxes.

HBACK-AJ2